Roses of the West

of the

Other non-fiction books
by Anne Seagraves

Daughters of the West © 1996

Soiled Doves: Prostitution In The Early West © 1994

High~Spirited Women Of The West © 1992

Women Who Charmed The West © 1991

Women Of The Sierra © 1990

Tahoe, Lake In The Sky © 1987

Beautiful Lake County © 1985

Roses of the West

By Anne Seagraves

Copyright © 2002 by WESANNE PUBLICATIONS
Printed in the United States of America

Published by WESANNE PUBLICATIONS
Post Office Box 428
Hayden, Idaho 83835

Library of Congress Control Number 2002090306
ISBN 0-9619088-6-6

ACKNOWLEDGMENTS

COVER PHOTO:
Author's Collection

GRAPHIC DESIGNER: Sheila R. Bledsoe

Arizona Historical Society, Tucson, AZ; Austin Historical Society, Austin, NV; Dechutes Historical Society, Bend, OR; Eastern California Museum, Independence, CA; F.M. Olin Library, Mills College, Oakland, CA; Georgia Historical Society, Macon, GA: Inyokern County Library, Bishop, CA; Laws Railroad and History Museum, Bishop, CA; Montana Historical Society, Helena, MT; Nevada City Chamber of Commerce, Nevada City, CA; Nevada Historical Society, Reno, NV; Northwest Museum of Arts and Culture, Spokane, WA; Ohio Historical Society, Columbus, OH; Old Trail Museum, Choteau, MT; Spellbinder Bookstore, Bishop, CA; University of Texas, Houston, TX; University of Washington, Manuscripts and Special Collections, Seattle, WA; University of Wyoming, State Archives Department, Laramie, WY; Wyoming State Department of Parks and Cultural Resources, Cheyenne, WY; Wallace Mining District Museum, Wallace, ID.

In researching Roses of the West, many individuals have been extremely helpful. The author would like to thank the following: Carl Halberg, Archivist, University of Wyoming, Laramie, WY; Jane Fisher, Bishop, CA; Lena Calvello, Sparks Little Theatre, Reno, NV; Rayette Wilder, Archives Library, Northwest Museum of Arts & Culture, Spokane, WA; R.J.M. Blackett, University of Texas, Houston, TX; Sharon McGowan, Librarian, Charles Russell Museum, Great Falls, MT.

AND A VERY SPECIAL THANK YOU TO THE FOLLOWING: Dorothy and Burton Devere, Rose Tree Museum, Tombstone, AZ, for providing family history and photos for the Ethel Robertson Macia story; Jim and Frances Salmond, Choteau, MT, for providing history and photos for the Elizabeth Smith Collins story; John Amonson, Wallace Mining District Museum, Wallace, ID, for sharing his photos of May Arkwright Hutton and the Hercules Mine; Genny Smith, Genny Smith Books, for sharing her book, *Dr. Nellie*, and making the story of Dr. Nellie MacKnight Doyle possible.

AND A VERY SPECIAL THANK YOU TO:

Bob Smith, Bookprinters Network, Portland, OR, for professional advice; Valle Novak, Ponderay, ID, for her fine editing; Sheila Bledsoe, Graphic Designer, Post Falls, ID, for her outstanding artwork throughout the book; and, as always, my husband, Wes, who has worked with me through the writing of this book.

FOREWORD

As the title of this book suggests, the rose was a symbol of the women of the early west: rare, precious, and difficult to find. Men often described their wives or sweethearts as beautiful as a rose, sweet as a rose, or gentle as a rose. Female rodeo stars had names like Texas Rose Bascom and Prairie Rose Henderson. Although the rose itself appears to be fragile, there are many varieties that are hardy and tenacious as well as beautiful — all attributes of the western woman.

The western woman was many things. She was a high-spirited cowgirl on a white horse rounding up cattle, a worn and faded house-wife in a gingham dress, or a dignified suffragette striving for women's rights. Whatever she was, she was independent.

In the mid-1830s, the industrialization of the northeastern United States nearly brought an end to home-based industries. The work-place became one of factories, shops, and businesses that valued pro-duction over people. When women could no longer work at home, they became lost in the new labor force, working 12 hours a day, often under abusive conditions, for a low wage. Overnight, the woman went from a respectable person to a second rate citizen, with no hope of improvement. Although many men were used to working outside the home, they too were affected by the changes. Several farmers found their land losing its value, and there was a lack of employment in the cities. Obviously, there was no future in the east for the common people.

Without hope of opportunity in their own area, men and women regarded the west as the new symbol for wealth and better lives. The first pioneers to venture over the treacherous trails were mostly men, with a few courageous women by their sides. By 1840, more women began traveling to the frontier with their husbands. And, as they struggled west, those women changed, becoming tough and resource-ful. It was as though they were preparing for what was ahead.

The first female pioneers rose to the challenges of the frontier, working beside their husbands to cultivate the land, as well as a new lifestyle. Those who lacked stamina when they arrived soon acquired it out of necessity. They wanted better lives than the ones they had left behind, and they were willing to work for them.

Since fate had forced those ladies into unfeminine roles, many began wearing male attire. They traded their cumbersome, long dresses for the comfort of trousers. This added a new freedom that was not shared with their sisters in the industrialized cities they had left behind.

As word spread in the east of the wealth of the frontier, other ladies also began escaping the constraints society imposed upon them. Soon women from all walks of life began to arrive. These newcomers were a welcome addition to the fast growing settlements. They became schoolteachers, dressmakers, ranchers, and boardinghouse keepers. Within a short time, a ladies aid society was formed and began taking care of destitute families and women in need. The men, without realizing it, were no longer the dominant force; they found themselves sharing equal status with the women. Many of them resented it; others packed up and moved away to start again in a male society.

By 1880, the women who journeyed west realized they were a scarcity in this new land, where they were sought after and appreciated. Those ladies were able to enjoy more freedoms, and they nearly started a revolution when they insisted upon houses with floors, instead of hovels and shacks.

Women missionaries, ladies of medicine, and suffragettes were also moving to the territory. It seems American women had seized the opportunities the west offered, and although historians rarely recorded it, these ambitious females had risen to the heights of great achievement.

*Today, as the women of tomorrow stand
on the threshold of a new era, it is
hoped the despairs of the past will be
replaced with the promises of the future.*

CONTENTS

Cover Photo Author's Collection

Valle Novak, Editor
Sheila R. Bledsoe, Graphic Designer

INTRODUCTION

With the opening of the American frontier, thousands upon thousands of men, women, and children traveled west to begin new lives. Although many of their dreams would come true, just as many were left in the dust. During that period, the female pioneers took time from their busy lives to keep diaries and records. It was from the pens of those women that historians uncovered a part of yesterday's legacy for the future.

There was something about the early west that inspired people to attempt great things; the women in this book followed that pattern. Their individual stories span a time period from 1825 through the turn-of-the-century — no two women were alike.

Elizabeth Collins, who was born in 1844, was one of the adventurous pioneers who helped to settle the west. During her lifetime, this spunky lady was captured by the Indians and held prisoner for six months. When she was finally released, she went on to become a cattle rancher. In 1889, she was the first woman to successfully ship her own livestock by rail to the markets of the East.

In Wyoming, the dedicated Nellie Tayloe Ross was the first lady to be elected governor in the nation. When her term was over, the active Mrs. Ross went on to become the first woman director of the United States Mint. Before she retired, Nellie was known as a "cracking good governor," and affectionately called "Our Nell" by the taxpayers.

In 1859, a little girl named Emma was singing for coins in the doorways of both Nevada City, California, and Austin, Nevada. That child went on to become the famous Emma Nevada, the first western woman to gain prominence in the difficult medium of grand opera. Emma entertained the royal heads of Europe and was the first unofficial ambassador from the West.

While Miss Nevada performed in Europe, the lively Kate Rockwell was entertaining the gold-happy miners in the rich Yukon Territory. Although Kate was the undisputed "Queen of the Yukon," she left it all behind to homestead a ranch in the high country near Bend, Oregon. Miss Rockwell is considered to be one of the last of the old-time pioneers of the West.

In Tombstone, Arizona, "the town too tough to die," Ethel Macia, at the age of 14, had to assume the responsibility of raising four younger siblings. She not only succeeded, but also became known as a guardian of other children and respected for her many acts of kindness.

The same year Ethel was raising her little family, 17-year-old Nellie MacKnight Doyle, from Bishop, California, was battling her way through medical school, in an era when women just didn't do that sort of thing. Despite the insults she received from the male professors, who firmly believed all female doctors were failures, Nellie walked out of the college with a medical degree. She returned to Bishop and spent the next 25 years saving lives in the Owens Valley.

During the early 1900s, the unconventional May Hutton hitched her wagon to a star in northern Idaho, and became a millionaire when the famous Hercules Mine came in. Although the boisterous lady often shocked "proper" women, she definitely knew how to spend her money. Without hurting her own lifestyle, May shared her wealth with the needy, while dedicating her time to suffrage in both Idaho and Washington.

Perhaps the most touching story in this book is that of Ellen Craft, a slave. She was fathered by her master when he forced himself upon her mother, and then, as a "yard child," she was abused by her mistress. Ellen's desperate flight to freedom will grab every heart — the end of her story will make the reader pause a minute and think!

Although not all of these women were movers and shakers, they were all part of the fascinating history of the American West. These ladies represent a time that is no more, and serve as an inspiration to those who follow.

The stories of these remarkable women have been carefully researched and documented through the generous assistance of historians, librarians and the special collection departments of many leading universities.

I have spent years reading old, out-of-print books, biographies, newspapers dating from the mid-1800s to the mid-1900s, magazines, diaries, personal letters, public records, and correspondence.

As with all history, one must rely upon what others have written or recorded. In this book, I have attempted to create readable, accurate stories of the women of yesterday and their achievements.

— The Author

Elizabeth Smith Collins
Elizabeth lived the life of a pioneer
with all its struggles and hardships.

Chapter 1

ELIZABETH SMITH COLLINS
THE CATTLE QUEEN OF MONTANA

Elizabeth Collins was one of the adventurous pioneers who helped to settle the early west. During her eventful life she was many things: wife, mother, cattlewoman, and most importantly, a friend to those in need. Elizabeth's courage and many acts of kindness burned like a candle in the wilderness, leading the way for others to follow.

Elizabeth (Libby) Smith was born in 1844, in Rockford, Illinois. She was the ninth child of Solomon and Elizabeth Davis Smith. A tenth and last child, Chan, was born later.

Mr. and Mrs. Smith were dedicated parents who raised their children to be self-sufficient, independent adults. Although money was usually scarce in the Smith's home, there was never a shortage of love and understanding. As Libby grew up in this caring environment, she developed confidence in herself and the ability to survive the perils of life in the West.

At an early age, Libby learned to chop wood, haul water and help her mother with the never-ending piles of dirty laundry. In her autobiography, Libby described herself as the family roustabout, but admitted that a less active, more humdrum life would have been boring. She enjoyed working and found even the simplest task a challenge.

When Libby was ten years old, her family left Illinois and settled for a brief time in what is now known as Madison, Iowa. A short time later, her father joined the great tide of emigrants sweeping toward the west. He was a hard-working, adventurous man who was always searching for a better life. It was this legacy he passed on to his youngest daughter.

In May 1855, the Smith family took their place in the long line of covered wagons headed for Denver, Colorado. There were hundreds of miles to travel and many hardships ahead, but the party seemed unconcerned; they were filled with optimism and cheer as they left Iowa. Libby was the only young girl, and she was looking forward to the new venture as much as her father. At eleven, Libby was a sturdy child with a sprinkling of freckles across her nose and a smile that brought joy to all who knew her.

As the wagons bumped and rolled toward the frontier, the travelers endured dust storms, overflowing rivers, and often a shortage of supplies. Their long, hard trip, however, was no different from the ones others had made before them, including the terrible fear of an Indian attack. The men were well armed and constantly on guard, watching for any signs of trouble. A few weeks into the journey their fears were realized.

In her autobiography, Libby gave a description of their encounter with what is believed to be the Sioux. She was standing at the edge of camp helping prepare the evening meal when she noticed they were surrounded by a band of Indians. Although the warriors seemed peaceful, the women immediately fled for the shelter of their wagons. When Libby attempted to follow, she found someone had grasped her tightly around the waist. Without thinking, she instinctively gave whomever it was a ringing slap across his face, and to her horror, found it was the chief's son — and he was outraged. No female had ever before dared to strike the son of a chief.

The entire camp was stunned, for a blow to a warrior was the greatest insult imaginable. When the chief rode up to see what had happened, he saved the day by taking the insult as a joke. Indians admired courage above all, and to the chief the sight of his angry son glaring down at a young white girl who was glaring back must have been funny. Soon after, the warriors rode out of the camp along with the young male offender, who failed to see any humor in his loss of dignity. At that time, Libby had no idea how lucky she was — nor did she know then that she and the chief would meet again, only under different circumstances.

After six hard weeks of travel the settlers finally reached their destination, only to be disappointed. One day Denver would be known as "The Queen City of the West," but in 1855, it was just another collection of shanties and small cabins with the usual saloons and general store. It was there the Smiths made their home.

For the next few years, Libby's father worked when he could and spent the rest of his time prospecting for gold in Colorado and the surrounding territories. When news of a rich strike in New Mexico spread throughout the area, he joined a group of adventurers in hopes of finding his fortune. Sadly, this trip, like all the others, was futile. Soon after his return from New Mexico, Libby lost her father, and a short time later, her mother. She was left alone at 16, in a town where men outnumbered the women 100 to one, and shootings were a daily occurrence. It was time to return to the rest of her family.

One of Libby's brothers was a freighter with a caravan heading east, and she decided to travel with him to Iowa. Libby, however, was not destined to leave the west. After several hundred miles of travel, she and her brother separated from the main caravan to visit a settler. There had not been any signs of Indians for days and they felt safe from attack, but they were mistaken. At just about dusk, a large band of warriors sprang from cover, and within minutes the pair was surrounded. Libby's brother fought desperately to save her, and failed. The last thing she saw was the sight of him being knocked to the ground by a large club — she later wrote she believed her brother was dead.

The Indians dragged Libby from her horse, blindfolded her, then started to travel, walking all night without sleep. When the blindfold was removed she saw there were other captives. One, a white woman with six children, was in need of help, but when Libby tried to assist she was threatened with an ax. All the captives were given food and water before the journey continued. As Libby started to walk with the rest, a warrior on a pony came up beside her and, to her surprise, pulled her up with him.

At first Libby didn't know why she had been favored. Later, when she was able to turn around, she found it was the chief whose son she had slapped several years earlier. He had admired her courage then, and now decided she should become his possession. A chill ran up Libby's spine and she was filled with a terror she knew she had to hide — the chief wanted her because she was brave — no matter what happened the young woman knew she couldn't disappoint him.

When they reached camp that night, the warriors began to fight over possession of the prisoners. Libby stayed close to the chief and he led her away to his tepee, removed the binding from her wrists, and placed her in the care of his daughter. Libby passed the night in safety, while listening to the desperate screams of the other captives.

The next morning when they broke camp the remaining prisoners could hardly walk. Libby again rode on the same pony in front of the chief. The other members of the tribe seemed angry and she was afraid, but again the chief claimed Libby as his own, and eventually the rest of the braves left her alone.

For almost five months Libby remained under the chief's protection, sleeping nightly in the safety of his tepee. During that time she had to watch the torture the rest of the captives endured, always in fear that someday the chief would not be able to keep her safe. His son was her worst enemy, as he hated her and made every effort he could to cause pain. Finally, the day arrived when the chief could no longer defend Libby — the tribe insisted that she had to run the gauntlet, and he reluctantly agreed.

The gauntlet was a deadly sport in which a prisoner was forced to fight his way through a line of uplifted tomahawks and clubs. The most honored warrior had the privilege of being at the head of the line. If he could be the first to strike the fatal blow, more honor was bestowed upon him.

During her captivity, Libby had been forced many times to observe the terrified prisoners running and fighting their way through the gauntlet. It had been sickening to see them and not be able to help, but she did notice the faster a person ran, the better his chance of survival. When her turn came, Libby hesitated, then looked at the chief, took a deep breath, and ran at top speed in the fight of her life.

The Indians were taken by surprise for a moment. They were used to terrified people who fell to their knees, unable to stand, not a strong, young woman who was determined to live. Their delay saved Libby's life; it gave her a chance to make it almost to the end before she received a hard blow to her head from a hatchet.

Libby fell to the ground unconscious. She remained near death for two weeks. When she awoke she was in the care of the chief's daughter. In a few days she was walking, and at that point Libby wondered if any of the surviving captives would ever be rescued.

When a war party returned a few days later bringing with them several of their own dead, Libby saw a piece of blue cloth in the hand of a lifeless warrior; she knew then that help was near, and she was right. The following day a company of soldiers rode into camp demanding an exchange of prisoners. The chief approached Libby and asked her to remain with him. She hesitated a minute, not wishing to offend him, for he had been kind. Then she pretended she was sorry to leave as an officer led her away. This saved the chief's dignity. Later, Libby found her brother was alive and a member of the company that rescued her.

Libby had been a captive for six months. During that time she began to hate Indians. Later, as her natural love of all people returned, she knew it wasn't the Indians she hated, it was their acts of violence that were evil. She also realized it was their way of life, and in her heart Libby knew the white people were no doubt as guilty, in their own way, as the Indians.

After her release from captivity, Libby returned to Denver with her brother. When he went back to work with the Overland Freight, Libby signed on as a camp cook. There were approximately 60 men to feed, quite an undertaking for a 17-year-old girl. She later wrote in her autobiography, ". . . and for many a long hard week, month and year thereafter, my home was the wide far-reaching plains and my abode the canvas covered wagon in a freight train."

Libby made 12 long, tedious trips from the Missouri River to the Rocky Mountains. "The men," she wrote, "were rough, uneducated, and unrefined, but not a word of an insulting nature did I receive." During those years, she encountered dust so thick it was often hard to breathe, flooding rivers, and blizzards that made traveling difficult. It was not unusual for her to wake up to find several inches of snow on her blankets and below zero temperatures outside.

Although Libby's skin turned brown from the hot sun and her hands became rough and blistered, she always retained her femininity. There would be a piece of lace, a ruffle at her throat, or a flower pinned upon her shoulder. Her smile was as engaging as ever and to her life was still an exciting adventure.

On Libby's last trip with the Overland Freight, there was a serious Indian attack and several men were killed. The wagon master decided to divide the train at Crazy Woman's Fork; Libby was chosen to act as one of the scouts. She was well qualified for she had spent a great deal of her life prospecting with her father. Libby piloted the party safely across the Big Horn at Fort Smith, on through Yellowstone, and to the present site of Bozeman. From there they went to Virginia City, Montana, where both brother and sister left the train. It was the fall of 1863; Libby was 19 years old.

Virginia City was a place of crime, violence, and lawlessness. The town was bursting out in all directions and most of the inhabitants were filled with dreams of gold and get-rich-quick schemes. Housing was scarce, so Libby and her brother immediately prepared a shelter for the winter.

They built a small, low cabin from charred pine logs, with holes for a door and window. The floor was earth, so Libby covered it with a carpet of buffalo hides pinned down with stakes. A sheet-iron stove was used for cooking and light was furnished by candles. A box, a rough stand, homemade table, and improvised beds completed the furnishings. It was warm and comfortable.

A few weeks after they moved in, Libby's brother became seriously ill and unable to work, leaving his sister to earn their living. Everything was expensive, especially food. The deep snows of 1863-1864 kept provisions from being shipped in. During that winter, a 100-pound sack of flour cost $110, potatoes were 60 cents a pound, and eggs $2.50 a dozen.

At first Libby cleaned and cooked for the miners, but soon realized that more money was needed. When she heard that a tailor, who had located there, wanted to return to England for a visit, she managed to rent his sewing machine for seven dollars a month. Libby opened the first dressmaking parlor in the territory conducted by a woman, and soon had almost more business than she could handle.

In addition to working for individuals, she secured a contract to sew flour sacks for five cents each. By diligent work she could turn out 100 sacks a day. In this way Libby earned enough to support both herself and her brother until he recovered.

During this time Libby became a great favorite with the miners because of the many little things she did for them. She helped the ill and injured because she hated to see people suffer, and was never too busy to sew a button on a shirt. In this manner, Libby became a loved and respected citizen of Virginia City. That holiday season the men decided to do something special for her. When she opened the door on Christmas morning she found a 100-pound sack of flour with a note, "Merry Christmas from the miners." Needless to say, it was a most welcome gift, and one she would never forget.

In the spring, her brother recovered enough to take over some of the responsibilities. By that time they had both begun to hate the lawlessness of the turbulent town. Although Libby had never been molested in any way, many other women had. There was a great need for law and order that would protect women from insults and end the senseless shootings. For this reason dedicated men of like mind banded together and formed the famed Montana Vigilantes.

In her autobiography, Libby wrote, "As if by magic, the face of society was changed within a few short weeks; for it was soon known that in tones that might not be disregarded, the voice of Justice had spoken. Holding in one hand the swift-descending and inevitable sword of retribution, and in the other the invisible, yet effective shield of protection, the Vigilantes warned the thief to steal no more, commanded the brawler to cease from strife, and struck from his nerveless grasp the weapon of the assassin." It was obvious Libby was delighted. She had a great admiration for the Vigilantes and the work they did — at that time, she had no idea she would someday marry a man who had been a member of this elite group.

In the spring of 1864, Libby and her brother moved to another mining camp 15 miles from Virginia City. He went to work in the mines and Libby took in boarders. When her brother decided to return to Denver, she moved to Bannock to work as a nurse and housekeeper for an older woman. A few months later she left that job to work for a doctor, receiving a salary of $25 a week, which was considered a large wage in those days.

During the following years, Libby lived in various mining camps in Madison County and Helena. In the spring of 1874, when she was 30 years old, Libby became a cook at a mining camp near Silver City. It was there she met and fell in love with Nathaniel Collins, the owner of a silver mine. Nathaniel (Nat) was a man Libby could both love and respect. He had fought with the Eleventh Illinois Volunteers during the Civil War, and at one time had been a member of the Vigilantes.

Nat's love for Libby was obvious. The couple married on New Year's Eve, 1874, in Helena. Following a brief honeymoon, they returned to Silver City to live near the mine. Nat had furnished his home especially for Libby, and as a surprise he had purchased a cow for $75. Libby was quite proud of that gift for it was an achievement to own a cow in those days. That present from Nat was the foundation of the Collins' herds that would someday become familiar on the ranges of northern Montana.

In 1877, Libby and Nat decided to raise livestock instead of mining silver. Nat sold his business and bought a small ranch eight miles from Silver City. The couple's first herd consisted of Libby's cow and 150 head of cattle, which carried the brands "C" for Collins and "77," taken from the Vigilante code.

The numbers 3-7-77 have a special meaning in Montana. When the Vigilantes hung a criminal, it was said that he was buried in a grave three feet wide, seven feet deep, and seventy-seven inches long. Those same numbers that represented law and order in the early west are carried on today. In 1956, the numbers 3-7-77 were placed on the Montana Highway Patrol's shoulder patch and the car door insignia as a tribute to the "first people's police force." Although the Vigilantes have been gone for many years, their symbol of law and order lives on today.

Nat and Libby remained near Silver City for three years. During that time the winters were so severe that in 1880, they moved their herd to the beautiful Teton Valley. Nat purchased 600 acres of land in what was then called Old Agency, later to become Choteau. Their new home was a small log cabin situated on the banks of the Teton River. At that time settlers were scarce. Most of the inhabitants were Blackfoot Indians, who had lived there all of their lives, and they welcomed the new family.

Libby had overcome her fear of Indians many years before, and soon became good friends with her neighbors. She shared her medical skills with the Blackfoot, and in return they taught her how to create their intricate beadwork. Within a few months Libby learned to speak their language fluently. In 1881, Mrs. Collins gave birth to a daughter, Carrie, who was welcomed and loved by all. Carrie was the first white child to be born in the Valley of the Teton.

During the next few years, Nat and Libby's herd grew and prospered; soon there were thousands of cattle upon their range. Libby rode beside her husband, working as hard as any ranch hand. She grew fond of the lonely cowboys and was always willing to listen to their problems, as well as lend a hand to those in need. For years there wasn't a doctor in the slowly growing community, and "Aunty Collins," as she was known, looked after the sick and injured. It was not unusual to see Libby run out in the middle of the night, swing up behind a rider on a galloping horse, and race across the county to help some poor suffering soul. She could set a broken arm or leg, and, if necessary, bring a child into the world. No one knows how many babies Aunty Collins helped to deliver.

When her husband developed poor health, Libby took over the business of raising stock. At that time buyers would come to the ranch to bargain for cattle, but in 1889, Libby decided to take the herds to the eastern markets herself and increase their earnings. Since women of that era weren't supposed to ride on the train with the cattlemen, it was not to be an easy task.

After driving her first shipment of livestock 90 miles over the plains to Great Falls, the railroad officials flatly refused to let Libby ride in the caboose with the ranchmen. They claimed it was against the regulations. At that point, Mrs. Collins became angry and vowed she would ride on that train or die trying.

For ten days she telegraphed back and forth, finally, when her friends, the stockmen, threatened to boycott the railroad, she won her victory. As the triumphant Libby Collins stepped into the caboose, a cowboy waved his hat and yelled, "Three cheers for Aunty Collins, the 'Cattle Queen of Montana,'" and the name stuck.

In 1890, Libby wrote her autobiography; unfortunately, there were only 1,000 copies printed. The book, which described her personal history along with life in the west, was so well received that Libby began lecturing around the country, becoming an early-day publicist. The audiences were so interested in her experiences and descriptions of the west, they began to visit the area, and the merchants prospered. The Great Falls Business Men's Association was so pleased they requested the merchants of that city, and the surrounding area, to welcome Mrs. Collins with liberal discounts. She had become a celebrity.

As Libby's popularity grew, the larger newspapers became interested in her career. In November 1894, *The Mountaineer* wrote the following article, "On the stage, cattle queens are addicted to flapping sombreros and buckskins, but the real cattle queens dress in comfortable gray gowns, have round jolly faces and are as slippery as eels when requested to talk about themselves. At least that is the impression carried away by a *Daily News* reporter who tried this morning to interview Mrs. Collins, the Cattle Queen of Montana, who is in Chicago with her shipment of stock, the first woman to come here on that mission."

Libby enjoyed publicity when it came to the livestock business, but was both evasive and humorous when quizzed about her personal life. When one newsman asked her how she felt, her answer was, "How do I feel? As well as any Montana person used to miles of fresh air can feel when tucked up in a forty-story room, where you have to light the gas to do your hair."

Another time, when a reporter asked her how she escaped from the Indians, she replied in her easy way, "Oh, I was full of the old

Harry in those days and I ran away — or else I suppose I would be there yet. No I can't tell you about it, haven't time." Then, with her hearty laugh, she would continue to bargain over the cattle, while at the same time learning the latest methods of branding.

Mrs. Collins was proud of her herds; when she and Nat first started the business they knew how many head of cattle they owned. In 1894, they no longer bothered to count. Their livestock was well known and in demand throughout the nation.

During her years working the cattle, Libby had gained a reputation as one of the best informed stock people in the business. She knew the market prices and had the ability to deal with men without creating hostility. Libby was a fair woman, who was respected by all who knew her.

The Collins' home had always been a happy one. As their daughter Carrie grew up, the sounds of her laughter rang through the house. Carrie was never lonely; she had many playmates in the valley, along with two little orphaned Blackfoot girls that Libby and Nat adopted and raised as their own. She attended school in Choteau and at the age of 23, Carrie Collins and Frank Salmond, a prominent rancher, were united in marriage.

Libby and Nat retired from the livestock business a few years later, and moved into Choteau, which had grown into a prosperous little city. Libby, however, didn't take long to declare that she was not a "rocking-chair" woman. For a brief time she became involved in mining. In 1908, when she heard about the rich gold strikes in Alaska, she made a trip to that area in search of adventure, and perhaps a little gold. At that time, Libby was 64 years old.

Nathaniel Collins passed away in December 1911, at the age of 77. After the loss of her husband, Libby increased her commitments to community affairs and the schools of Choteau. For a while she continued to travel on occasional lecture tours. As time passed, Libby began spending her winters in the warmer climate of California.

In 1921, Elizabeth Smith Collins died in Choteau, following a lengthy illness. She had lived a full, eventful life, but was not unwilling, when the time came, to pass on to the next frontier, beyond the Divide.

The site of Nat and Libby's original homestead in the beautiful Teton Valley of Montana.

Ear Mountain can be seen in the background.

Although Elizabeth and Nathaniel Collins have been gone for many years, their legacy is alive and thriving in the Valley of the Teton. Today, on the site of the original home ranch, livestock bearing the "two circle," the "C," and the "77" brands, graze peacefully on the large Salmond spread. Here, in this fertile valley, the past has merged gracefully with the present, where it can continue on through the generations yet to come.

Elizabeth Smith Collins

Nat Collins

Mrs. Nat "Libby" Collins, Chan Smith her brother (on left), Nat Collins (with beard), and Carrie Collins (daughter)

Carrie Collins
The first white child born in the Teton Valley

Excerpts from *The Cattle Queen of Montana*
By Elizabeth Collins

Elizabeth was surrounded by the cowboys who worked the ranch, many of whom she befriended. She listened to their troubles, cared for them when they were ill, and lent them money when they were broke. In her autobiography she wrote:

"I am prepared to say that the Montana cowboy is a fair-minded, noble-hearted, generous and whole-souled [sic] man. Many are the poor boys whose broken arms and limbs I have bandaged as they lay upon rocks or dry hard earth of the prairie, far from home or habitation, where they had been injured by a vicious horse or enraged animal and in this manner I earned the title of "Aunty" or "Mother" and in possession of such cognomens I cannot but feel exceeding pride, for I have learned to look upon these boys, now that I know them so well, as true types of manly courage, generosity, and activity."

"The young cowboys, as a rule, were bright, active, intelligent young men, generous, liberal to a fault and withal possessed of many noble qualities. True it is, there were some worthless, low and degraded men among their number, but those of this character constituted but a small minority."

"I may be peculiar in my likes and dislikes — cranky in the opinion of the cod-fish aristocracy — but, nevertheless, I would rather today be the "Aunty" or "Mother" and "Cattle Queen of Montana" than sit upon the throne of a real queen."

Excerpts from *The Cattle Queen of Montana*
By Elizabeth Collins

Elizabeth dwelt in the shadow of the gallows. As she traveled the streets of the turbulent town of Virginia City, Montana, she knew a Vigilante Committee was being organized. At last, something was going to be done to protect the decent people. In her book, Elizabeth described those lawless days of that era.

"One of the chief evils of those early days was the saloon; the other, absence of good female society. Women of easy virtue were always present in large numbers, habited in the most costly and attractive apparel, brazen-faced and bold, promenading the streets and receiving fabulous sums for their purchased favors. Public gambling houses are on every street, with open doors and loud music, and are resorted to in broad daylight by hundreds; and as a matter of course, these places furnish a fruitful source of crime, inasmuch as all quarrels are commonly decided on the spot by appeal to brute force, the stab of a knife, the discharge of a revolver."

"In fact, all the temptations to vice are present and on full display with money in abundance to secure the gratification of the mountaineer — the desire for novelty and excitement. . . ."

"In his wildest excitement, a mountaineer respects a woman and anything like an insult offered to a lady would be resented by any bystanding [sic] miner. For the preservation of those sacred rights and customs and maintenance of these, the Montana Vigilantes banded together."

There is little doubt that Elizabeth was eager for some form of protection from the evil of that city.

THIS UNHEEDED VIGILANTE WARNING, PRESENTED TO AUSTIN LYNCH BY
DR. CLARK OF BROOKLYN, CAUSED THE LYNCHING OF CON MURPHY, NOTORIOUS
OUTLAW AT HELENA, MONTANA TERRITORY IN 1884.

Courtesy of the Montana Historical Society

Vigilante Skull and Crossbones

The Mystery of 3-7-77

In the 1860s, lawlessness and violence in the Montana Territory became so overwhelming that the citizens of Virginia City formed a "vigilante committee." Within a few days a small group of dedicated, armed horsemen rode out, and within forty-four days, twenty-one troublemakers and murderers were hanged. The next few years the people enjoyed a relatively peaceful life.

During that time the numbers 3-7-77 appeared as a symbol or code of the vigilantes. Although historians know the numbers 3-7-77 stand for law and order, there has been a considerable amount of controversy as to the year they first appeared, and why the numbers 3-7-77 were chosen — today those questions linger.

One theory is that the numbers were a warning of banishment from the community. The deadline for the ill-fated person to leave being three hours, seven minutes, and seventy-seven seconds. Translated that would be three hours, eight minutes, and seventeen seconds.

Another explanation surfaced in 1974, when an historian felt the numbers three and seven might have significance in Masonry. The numbers seventy-seven go back to an occurrence in 1862, which is part of Masonic history in Montana. In that year, a Freemason on his deathbed requested a Masonic funeral. When seventy-six Masons arrived for the ceremony, they counted the man in the coffin, making it seventy-seven.

The popular interpretation, however, is that when a criminal was hanged by the vigilantes he was buried in a grave three feet wide, seven feet deep, and seventy-seven inches long. But even this has a flaw; few men of that era were large enough to require a grave that size. . . .

Miss Emma Nevada

In 1880, the night of her debut at
Her Majesty's Theatre, London, England

Chapter 2

EMMA "NEVADA" WIXOM
"THE COMSTOCK NIGHTINGALE"

Emma Nevada left the rough mining camps and towns of California and Nevada to become one of America's most celebrated daughters. She was the first western woman to gain prominence in the difficult medium of grand opera. Although the capitals of Europe claimed Emma as their own, the talented lady usually ended performances with the song, "Star of Nevada," often with tears in her eyes.

On February 7, 1859, Emma Wixom was born in a crudely constructed log cabin at Alpha Diggings, a gold camp above Nevada City, California. Her father, Dr. "Bill" Wixom, and his wife, a former dealer in a gambling hall, were delighted with the perfect little girl. Both parents knew from the first there was something special about their child. And, they were right — Emma *was* special.

The winsome little girl sang almost as soon as she could talk. While Dr. Wixom waded through the heavy snows of the Alpine country attending to the ill and injured, his daughter began to laugh and imitate the sounds of the birds. As she grew into a toddler, Emma wandered across the road to the blacksmith's where she sang to the beat of his anvil. The neighbors soon began to gather outside the Wixom cabin to listen to the amazing child. All marveled at the sweetness of her voice.

By the time she was four, Emma, who was never shy or timid, was making public appearances and singing at local events. During the Fourth of July celebration someone draped the American flag around the small child and placed her upon a table where, to everyone's delight, she sang the National Anthem. It was said she never missed a word.

Emma's voice began to attract the attention of the weather-beaten miners who missed their own families. These lonely men would coax the little girl to sing for them, and in return tossed gold coins at her feet. They called for song after song and the tiny girl tried to comply with their wishes.

When the mines around Nevada City began to fail, Dr. Wixom decided to move his family to Austin, Nevada, which at that time, was an up and coming place. He opened an office for his medical practice and purchased a small horse ranch outside of the town. Austin provided more opportunities for the Wixoms and Emma was delighted with the friendly new faces. The citizens soon became used to seeing the little girl in a gingham dress, singing in doorways along the main street. As Emma grew older she made many friends and enjoyed a normal, happy childhood. The family blended into the community and became an integral part of the town.

Emma continued entrancing people with her music; at the age of seven, she sang at the dedication of the new Methodist Church, a place she learned to love. Her clear voice could be heard ringing out in the choir on Sundays and at most social affairs.

Life, however, was not to be all happiness. When Emma reached the early teens her mother passed away, leaving Dr. Wixom the responsibility of being both father and mother. As they shared their mutual grief Dr. Wixom and his daughter grew very close. The doctor was a stern but loving man who made Emma realize she had to develop her priceless talent. She learned to put her singing before everything else.

Shortly after her mother's death, the local music teacher took over the young woman's training, and the demand for Emma's appearances grew. She began performing throughout central Nevada and people came from all over to hear her sing — in a small way, Emma Wixom was already becoming famous.

Austin, with its over 6,000-feet altitude and clean air, provided a healthy environment for Emma's voice. With her father's help, she learned how to handle the horses and became an excellent horsewoman. She would ride over the mountain trails singing loudly, expanding and exercising her lungs. Singing was as natural to Emma as breathing.

When Emma completed her primary education, Dr. Wixom enrolled his daughter at Mrs. Mills Seminary in California (now Mills College). Although music was her main discipline, she also excelled in other subjects. Mrs. Mills became quite fond of the young woman and encouraged her to add foreign languages to her studies. Before she graduated Emma spoke seven languages fluently. No other opera star of that era ever equaled her linguistic ability. Emma wanted to be the best. When she performed she felt the full value of the words and meaning in the language it was written. Each opera was special to Emma, and she was special to her audiences.

The time spent at Mills Seminary was demanding. In later years Emma would be remembered by her classmates for her great talent, outgoing personality, and tiny figure. The students affectionately called her "Little Wixy," a name that remained with Emma the rest of her life. But keeping that tiny figure was a constant battle. She watched her weight carefully while working hard to develop her voice and style. All that dieting was worth it, however, as the exquisite Victorian costumes flowed gracefully over Emma's slender form. She had an air of elegance other stars often envied.

While at Mills Emma met Professor Ebell, a Yale graduate who had established a name for himself in the music and literary circles of Europe and America. He headed an organization known as the "International Academy," which sponsored talented students to study in Europe under his guidance. The professor was so impressed with Emma's dedication and voice that he invited her to join his group.

Emma was delighted with the offer. She also realized it would take a large sum of money. Dr. Wixom was not wealthy, but the chance to study music under the great Madame Marchesi, a noted teacher of the day, was something that was hard to turn down. Wixy returned to Austin to discuss the opportunity with her father. She knew if there was any possibility of accepting the professor's offer, he would find a way.

When Emma reached Austin she found there had been a terrible accident at one of the mines. A man she knew had been injured. This was a close community and many of her friends were organizing a benefit to help him. Emma joined in and offered to sing at the event and was immediately accepted. Everyone knew what a draw her voice would be.

The night of the affair Emma sang "Listen to the Mockingbird" for the first time in concert. Her voice was filled with so much compassion that tears streamed down the cheeks of the coarse miners. As Dr. Wixom listened carefully to his daughter, he silently vowed to do everything possible to help develop her career.

The following day the *Reese River Reveille* carried a glowing account of the fund-raiser and rave reviews of Emma's performance. The newspaper called her the "Comstock Nightingale" and added that she needed help to further her career. When the good citizens of Austin read the news, they dug deeper into their pockets to help finance Wixy. And Emma, at the age of 19, left for New York to join Professor Ebell. As the ship pulled away from the dock for Europe, no one knew that the Comstock Nightingale was destined to become one of the most recognized sopranos of her era.

A few days after reaching Liverpool, England, Professor Ebell suffered a fatal heart attack, abandoning his troupe on foreign shores. The turmoil that followed was devastating. The majority of the young people only understood English, and most were going to other countries to study. Since Emma spoke several languages she decided to go on alone.

Although she was terrified, Wixy traveled from Liverpool to Vienna to keep her scheduled appointment with the noted Madame Marchesi. During the audition her amazing voice exceeded the teacher's expectations and the two women, one a more than willing and apt student, the other a dedicated professional, went to work to expand the potential of Emma's great voice.

When Dr. Wixom received word of the professor's death he immediately left for Vienna to be with his daughter. Once again expenses were more than they had planned. It looked as though Emma might have to return home after all. But fate had other plans for the little diva. The Nevada newspapers carried stories of Ebell's death and Emma's dilemma. When Mrs. Marie Hungerford-Mackay, wife of the Comstock millionaire, read the news she remembered the little girl who once charmed the audiences of Nevada and she decided to sponsor the young woman. With Mrs. Mackay's wealth behind her, Emma's continued training was assured.

It was strange how the young protege and Mrs. Mackay had led similar lives. Both women had lived in the mining camps of the Mother Lode and silver towns of Nevada, and both had a burning desire — one to become a great opera star and the other a social leader. Their friendship grew into devotion and Mrs. Mackay became like a second mother to Emma.

Stories of Emma's successes were given celebrity status in the Nevada newspapers. Her career was followed with avid interest, especially in Austin. When Emma learned many operas in an unusually short period, the community was thrilled. When she was ready for her debut two years later, the townspeople were ecstatic, but not surprised. With dedication, natural talent, and a fine teacher, Emma had become a coloratura soprano of the finest quality and range.

Emma appeared in "La Sonnambula" for her debut at Her Majesty's Theatre in London, and she was triumphant. The enthusiastic audience shouted "Bravo" over and over; flowers were thrown at her feet. The little diva was called back to the stage several times as the people stood and kept applauding. At the time of her performance she chose "Emma Nevada" as her stage name, a name that was to become famous throughout both America and Europe.

The newspapers covered her debut and wrote: "In taking the name Emma Nevada, she hoped to do honor to both the state of Nevada and the city in California where she was born." The people of Austin had a huge party in honor of Wixy. During the celebration, a composer became so carried away he wrote a special tribute to the young woman, and the "Star of Nevada" was born. When Emma found out, she was so touched by his music that she often sang the song at the end of a performance.

Following her triumphant debut Emma appeared throughout Europe. Although she had a manager and Dr. Wixom to watch over her career, Emma felt she needed someone with more experience. While in England, she met Dr. Raymond Palmer and was immediately attracted to him. He was so smitten with her that he offered to give up his medical profession to become her manager. She accepted.

In 1885, Miss Nevada decided to embrace the Catholic faith. This was quite a shock to Emma's friends and completely out of character for the little star. Emma, however, had made up her mind. She was baptized at the Church of the Passionate Fathers in Paris, France. A special representative was sent from Rome to conduct the solemn ceremony and Mrs. Mackay became her godmother. Since Emma Nevada enjoyed star status, the media eagerly covered the important event. Stories and photos of the ceremony appeared around the world. Little Wixy, it seemed, had learned the value of publicity.

Although her popularity grew, Miss Nevada remained unaffected. She was a quiet, composed person, not headstrong or vain like many of the other stars. It was her nature to live simply. The royal heads of Europe purchased expensive tickets to hear the voice that was the talk of two continents, and these people continually sought Emma's company; she never sought theirs.

In August, 1885, the *Reveille's* headlines read: "The Lucky Lass of Austin," and announced the engagement of Emma Wixom to her manager, Dr. Raymond Palmer of Birmingham, England. The same article provided a description of her fiancee: "Dr. Palmer is but 28, and seems years older . . ." He is very tall, with great muscular strength, which is shown in his broad shoulders and strong limbs. He has a frank almost boyish countenance, and a rather florid complexion, pleasant blue eyes and light brown hair, and his manner is a well-bred cultivated Englishman." Unfortunately, other newspapers were not overly impressed with Dr. Palmer. One reported him as "fat and lazy with the coloring of a steak." Another described him as a "stage husband who wore gaudy jewelry." Wixy, who adored her husband-to-be, quietly ignored the less than complimentary reports.

The European newspapers were filled with stories of the forthcoming wedding. The following article of special interest was reprinted in the *Reveille*: "Instead of the regular engagement ring Miss Nevada wears a bracelet locked on one arm, and the doctor carries the key on his watch chain . . . the little prima donna, like all singers has a great many valuable jewels, a number having been given to her by her godmother Mrs. Mackay, the wife of the bonanza king; but she is more proud of the bracelet her lover locked on her arm than all of the others in her possession. . . ."

The prestigious wedding of Emma Wixom and Dr. Raymond Palmer took place at the English Embassy in Paris. It was followed by a second ceremony at the Church of the Passionate Fathers. The same representative who had officiated at Emma's baptism once again came from Rome to solemnize the joining of the two in holy matrimony. Following the wedding the happy couple immediately left for a honeymoon in Switzerland.

After their honeymoon Dr. and Mrs. Palmer and Bill Wixom left Europe for Miss Nevada's American tour. Emma desperately wanted to visit her own country, especially her friends in Austin. In order to do this the star had to turn down appearances in Madrid, London, and St. Petersburg and agree to visit the larger cities in the United States.

Her first performance was in Boston, then Philadelphia, Washington, Cleveland, and New York. Everyone was thrilled by the voice of the western star. The larger newspapers gave glowing accounts of Miss Nevada's remarkable talent and ability to charm both her audiences as well as the opera company that accompanied her.

When the troupe left New York for California Emma was aboard an elegant Pullman car named "Nevada." As news of the star's fame spread throughout the country, people stood in line to watch the brightly colored coach pass by. All were hoping to catch a glimpse of the prima donna within. Emma, however, was not up to par. Her schedule was too demanding. She developed neuralgia in New Orleans and had to have two teeth extracted. In St. Louis Wixy suffered from tonsillitis. Dr. Palmer was concerned and her manager was afraid Emma's voice would not be strong enough for the San Francisco appearance.

When the news media found out Miss Nevada was ill, they claimed she would not be at her best — but Emma had made up her mind a long time ago she would never let her audience down — and she didn't. In San Francisco the Comstock Nightingale's performance was outstanding. It was said her glorious voice was so full of passion it could be heard as far as the fifth floor of the Palace Hotel and filled the streets around the theatre. At the end of the concert, when Emma sang "Listen to the Mockingbird," the enthusiasm of the audience boardered on lunacy. They cheered and threw flowers at her feet, and she charmingly picked a huge bouquet to present to her music director.

During her stay in San Francisco, Miss Nevada became the idol of the California coast. Her rooms at the Palace were filled to capacity with many admirers unable to get near the star. She seemed at her best and concerns about her ill health were put to rest. While in the city, Emma, who had a sweet tooth, visited a special store. She became so fond of one candy that the store manager began calling them "Nevada Creams." The customers stood in line to buy the popular candy named after their favorite star.

Miss Nevada and her company bid farewell to San Francisco a few days later and boarded the train for two more stops. Although Emma was anxious to reach Austin, she was first scheduled to appear at Piper's Opera House in Virginia City.

As the train pulled into the station hundreds of fans were already on the platform waiting to greet the renowned diva. There were so many admirers that her manager was afraid she would get hurt in the excitement. Emma was rushed into a fancy coach and taken to the International Hotel. She rode down dusty streets where welcome signs were nailed on every door; Emma was happy to be home.

The next evening when the company arrived at the opera house, there were signs at the entrance that said: "Ladies are requested to leave their tall hats at home so that the people behind them can see Emma Nevada." As expected, the house was filled with Virginia City's elite. The sophisticated patrons of Piper's, who had heard the greatest voices of the day, were ready for an evening of entertainment.

When the curtain rose on the talented performers all eyes were riveted on Emma. She was dressed in an ornate gown and obviously very much in command. As her magnificent voice soared throughout the theatre, it was apparent why she was the toast of two continents. At the end of the opera the Comstock Nightingale sang "Star of Nevada," and the audience jumped to their feet applauding and screaming for another song. They did not want her to leave. Their namesake was all they had expected, and as all famous stars, she left them wanting more.

The next day the company left for Austin — the Wixoms were finally going home. Their train was met by a band playing a lively tune and a gaily decorated carriage, pulled by the young men of the town, was waiting to take them to their destination. Bonfires were on every street corner and hundreds of loyal supporters gathered to provide a welcome the family would never forget. Since the night was chilly, Emma didn't dare get out of the carriage. Instead, she pulled up the curtains and waved and threw kisses. It must have been a touching moment.

Emma, her husband, and Dr. Wixom were to stay at the home of the mayor and his wife during their visit in Austin. There was a special reception planned. Unfortunately, Miss Nevada could not participate, for she had to preserve her voice for the concert. Although Wixy was bursting with excitement and love on the inside, she had to remain silent. Dr. Wixom spoke for her and promised them his daughter would see all of her well-wishers after the performance.

As Emma and her company appeared on stage the next evening, she was wearing a rich costume sparkling with diamonds. A hush settled over the house. She stood quietly for a minute before beginning the most compelling performance of her life. And the people were treated to a night of music — and love — they would never forget.

As the sounds of her last aria faded, Emma held her arms out and sang "Home Sweet Home." There wasn't a sound in the theatre; absolute silence prevailed. When the applause began it was so violent it seemed the walls would collapse. Wixy was home and flowers came from all directions covering the star and stage. Finally the venerable form of Dr. Wixom rose from his chair and the audience joined him. One by one they stood and applauded both the doctor and his talented daughter.

When the theater quieted, Emma came forward and thanked everyone. She announced that she wished to be excused for a moment to change her dress and then hold an informal reception for as many as possible. She returned almost immediately and seating herself on the stage said: "Now I am just plain Emma Wixom." At that point Dr. Palmer, who had patiently been waiting in the background, asked to be introduced. Emma laughed and lovingly pulled her husband forward to meet her friends.

After the introduction, the couple handed out pieces of their wedding cake wrapped in white paper. Emma had carefully carried the cake from Europe to Austin in order to share a bit of her happiness with those she loved. Several hours later the last of the admirers left full of contentment and Emma's homecoming was complete.

In the morning a huge crowd escorted the company to a waiting train and watched them leave. It must have been hard for Dr. Wixom and Emma to say good-bye to their old neighbors and friends. Both surely hated to leave the town which was so full of memories. Emma did not know then that she would never see Austin again. Bill Wixom, however, remained in California and visited their old home many times before his death in 1888.

Emma and Dr. Palmer returned to Europe alone where she continued her career. A year later, the newspapers reported the Comstock Nightingale was going into semi-retirement. She and Dr. Palmer were expecting a child. When their daughter arrived they named her Mignon, after Emma's favorite opera. Both parents were thrilled and immediately began making plans for the baby's singing career. Mignon did not disappoint her parents. She went on to follow in her mother's footsteps, but she never did achieve the fame of Emma Nevada.

A year after Mignon's birth Emma returned to the stage. She had not lost her tiny figure and her voice was richer and more mature. It was said that the great Verdi traveled a thousand miles to persuade her to sing "Aida" in Italy, and it is assumed she did. As Emma's popularity increased, she caught the attention of Queen Victoria. Although the Queen never completely recovered from the death of her husband, Prince Albert, she did come out of mourning in

1887 while the empire celebrated the Golden Jubilee of her reign. Emma's great talent and quiet dignity appealed to the Queen who had a love of opera.

Later that year, Emma received the greatest honor accorded to any star, a Command Performance before the Queen of England. Although Miss Nevada was overwhelmed with emotion as she appeared before the austere Queen Victoria, her voice was never better. It was said the Queen was so delighted with the presentation that she placed a $100,000 diamond necklace around Emma's neck. The little star must have been deeply moved by Victoria's generosity for she treasured the gift above all others.

It was customary for the Queen to send a special invitation for High Tea to those she favored. When Emma received her embossed envelope with the message requesting her presence at the palace she was both excited and thrilled. Miss Nevada had enjoyed meeting the monarch and looked forward to seeing her again.

During the tea she was questioned about her life in America, and Emma, who was never at a loss for words, described the wonders of the west, Mills Seminary, and her home in Austin. Queen Victoria was enchanted by the honest little songstress and the two became friends.

Within a few weeks, Emma was invited to join the Queen's personal circle. She was enthusiastically accepted by the royalty. Little Wixy, with her charming personality, was a delight. She never failed to share the glory of her country and the beauty of both California and Nevada. In her own way Miss Nevada had become an unofficial ambassador from the West.

During the next few years, Emma was to return several times to America. In 1902, the star appeared in Nevada City and Mills College. In 1906, at the age of 47, she made a farewell tour, but there is no record of her returning to Austin. The Comstock Nightingale retired from the stage to live a quiet life. She gave voice lessons to a few select students and was devoted to her husband and daughter. Emma's home was always open to aspiring young musicians and many were helped with their careers.

In 1939, at the opening of the World's Fair on Treasure Island, E. Clampus Vitus proclaimed Emma Nevada the "Empress of Treasure Island." When she received the scroll with her title Emma was deeply touched. Her reply was that she only wished she could have been present for the ceremony.

On June 21, 1940, the great Emma Nevada was killed by a German bomb at her home in Liverpool, England. She was 81 years old. Her glorious voice was silenced forever.

Although both Lotta Crabtree and Jenny Lind have been written about in depth, it wasn't until Emma Wixom's death in 1940 that she was remembered, and then briefly. At that time it was said though she was in a different field of the art, Emma Nevada was to Austin what Mark Twain was to Virginia City. If her voice could have been recorded, her memory would have been as famous today as Mark Twain's writing.

Emma Wixom

Age five, taken at her family home in Nevada City, California

Emma Nevada, Mother Lode Nightingale
Wreaths of Flowers

"The following question has been asked: 'What was Emma Nevada's hobby, or did she have one?' For one thing, she liked to gather wild flowers and make wreaths of them, in the meantime sticking one or two of the blossoms in her hair.

If wild flowers were not obtainable she made her wreaths of domestic blossoms. On her head she would place the 'Wixom halo' and sing before the mirror.

In the earlier days Indian paint brushes made up the wreaths for Wixy's crowns. In later years one discovers her still making and wearing wreaths as headdresses in the operas she was destined to make famous. And when her beautiful daughter, Mignon, came along, she continued to make them for her. Then came a time later in her life when she wept tears of gladness because a wreath of early California poppies was presented to her at Nevada City. She never relinquished her fondness for flowers. One poet wrote this verse about her."

To the flowers you are kinship,
In your hair their wreaths entwine.
Like the ancient ones of laurel —
Laurels that are truly thine.

— Oakland Tribune, Sunday, September 8, 1940.

Courtesy of the Nevada Historical Society, Reno, Nevada

Emma "Nevada" Wixom
Mills Seminary, Circa 1876

Mills Hall, Circa 1900

Emma Nevada attended classes at Mills Seminary in the late 1870s.

Mills dates its founding as 1852, the year a Young Ladies Seminary was established at Bencia, California. In 1865, Cyrus and Susan Mills purchased the Seminary and began buying the acres of rolling farmland that were to become its present campus, which was then outside the small metropolis of Oakland.

The impressive Victorian-style Mills Hall was built, and the seminary moved to its new home in 1871. Mills became a college in 1885 — "It was the first and only chartered contemporary college west of the Rocky Mountains for women only." It granted its first college degree in 1889. Today, Mills is the only independent women's college among the many fine educational institutions in the San Francisco Bay Area.

— Excerpted from a Mills College brochure

Courtesy of Special Collections, F. W. Olin Library, Mills College

Mignon Nevada as "Ophelia."

Emma Nevada's New Engagement

Emma Nevada, Nee Emma Wixom, now Mrs. Palmer, will not chase the elegant dollar across the concert stage this season. She is now the member of a company composed exclusively of home talent. The youngest member thereof reaches high C with ease, warbles every night and gives encores without solication. She is about six weeks old and with her mama will find a private engagement in Paris all winter.

— *Reese River Reveille,* November 5, 1886

Emma Nevada's only child, Mignon, won distinction as a soprano in her own right under her mother's skillful tutelage. Although she inherited some of her mother's talent as a singer, Mignon never became as popular as the famous Emma Nevada. She did, however, develop her own style and appeared throughout Europe in well-known operas of the day, including her mother's favorite, "Mignon."

Mignon Nevada Palmer's Success

The recognition which music lovers of Europe have given to the gifted daughter of a gifted mother has been spontaneous and unstinted. It is the more interesting because Mlle. Mignon had spent her life in the musical circles of Europe excepting for the brief visits to America with her parents, she has had no musical instruction except her mother. At 13 she sang all her mother's operas in French, German and Italian as naturally as she did her exercises.

— Excerpted from *The San Francisco Call,* 1912

Courtesy of the Nevada Historical Society, Reno, Nevada

Emma Nevada

in the role of "Mignon"

THE GREAT EMMA NEVADA

Born Alpha Diggins, Nevada County, Cal. Feby. 7, 1859. Raised Austin, Nevada - Educated Mills Seminary. Died Wavertree, Liverpool, England, June 21, 1940. As world famous Prima Donna she climbed to heights of immortal fame; was honored by governments like no other woman of her time; on Bellini's statue at Naples rests her medallion; the great Gounod pronounced her "The Nightingale of Paradise." Her last appearance in the Comstock was at Piper's Opera House Thursday Dec. 3, 1885, in the Methodist Church at Austin on Dec. 5th. Her last tour of California, and home at Nevada City, where she sang at the age of 3, was in April 1902. She spoke 8 languages besides Piute, Washoe, and Shoshone; sang folklore songs of all nations in their mother tongues; appeared before all crowned heads of Europe, including Russia and Scandinavia; was a favorite of Queen Victoria who presented her with jewels valued over $100,000.00; lost all her property and possessions when Germans invaded Paris; died broken hearted and in poverty. Copyright - Burbank & Skyhawk

Courtesy of the Nevada Historical Society, Reno, Nevada

One of Emma Nevada's many post cards

Courtesy of the Nevada Historical Society, Reno, Nevada

"The Comstock Nightingale"
St. Petersburg, Russia

Emma Nevada Song Queen
Writes a Letter to the Press

"I have been asked to give the details of the regimen I follow on the day preceding an evening performance. In the first place I consider this point essential. I never talk anything above a whisper and speak as little as possible. I rise at 7:30, take a bath, then breakfast consisting of tea, bread and sirloin steak served at 8:30. Then I go to mass and afterward drive two horses and walk one hour. Fresh-air and exercise is [sic] very essential to me. I dine at 3, taking strong, clear broth with another sirloin steak, baked potatoes, roast chicken, but no salad, concluding with stewed prunes a baker apple and cream. I take one glass of good claret during the repast. After dinner I go to bed for two hours and try to sleep. I dress at home and usually arrive at the theatre five minutes before the curtain rises. After the performance I partake of supper composed of soup, beef and a glass of beer. I am very careful to avoid overheating, either in my rooms or dress. Never wear flannel underwear, relying greatly on health and strength not only on nourishing food but constant exercise in the open air.

To my young countrywomen who contemplate embracing the career of a professional singer I can only repeat what has already been said — they must study hard and patiently at least three years, must live well, as abundant and generous nourishment is necessary to sustain the strength of the student as well as that of the prima donna. Above all they should have funds for their support whilst awaiting engagements."

— *Reese River Reveille,* May 18, 1889 p.3

Ethel Robertson Macia

Chapter 3

ETHEL ROBERTSON MACIA
TOMBSTONE'S LADY OF THE ROSE

T he name Tombstone, Arizona, brings to life images of the days when the West was young and of a town that was considered too tough to die. Memories of the O.K. Corral, Boothill Cemetery and the infamous Bird Cage Theatre fill the mind, along with notorious men like Wyatt Earp, Doc Holliday, and Curly Bill. Although Tombstone was known as a place where lawlessness, gambling, and prostitution flourished, it was also a place where families raised their children and went to church on Sundays. And, it was there Ethel Robertson Macia, a lady who achieved success through the goodness within herself, was born and lived for 83 years.

ALICE

Ethel's story began in Leadville, Colorado, in 1880, when Alice Roberson, a lovely young woman of 16, and Chris Robertson, a mine foreman, were united in marriage. Three days after their wedding, the newlyweds joined a wagon train heading for Tombstone, Arizona. Tombstone's reputation as a new silver boomtown was spreading across the West, and Chris was confident he could make a better life for his new bride in that raw, wide-open town.

It took the Robertsons a little over two months to reach their destination. Although they traveled over 1,000 miles and endured the hardships of life on the trail, the young couple was so in love that all they could think of was being together. When they reached Tombstone, it was Christmas Eve and the sun was setting behind the Whetstone Mountains. As the last rays of light disappeared, Alice hugged her husband and told him how happy she would be when they had their new home. It was to be a year, however, before their house could be built. While she was waiting, Alice set up housekeeping in the wagon on an open lot because there was no other place available.

The couple's first home consisted of two rooms, and was built out of very rough, green lumber that was cut and hauled from the Chiracahua Mountains, 70 miles from Tombstone. It was never painted on the outside, and the inside walls were covered with cheese-cloth, which Alice papered. The house was sparsely furnished, cold in the winter and hot in the summer, but to the young bride it seemed a mansion. It was in that house that Ethel was born on August 6, 1881, the same year as the infamous shootout at the O.K. Corral.

Four years later Ethel's sister, Edith, arrived and the following year a brother, who died shortly after his birth. Although the young father worked hard to provide a good life for his family, there never seemed to be enough money. Everything was expensive and the mines in the surrounding areas appeared to be slowing down. Without jobs, many families were leaving to find employment elsewhere.

As Chris watched several of his friends pull out, he decided to try ranching. Their first place was a small house on 160 acres he homesteaded in the South Pass of the Dragoon Mountains. It was 16 miles from Tombstone, so the little family packed the old wagon and left, filled with high hopes of a better life.

Chris bought dairy cows and after a few weeks he established enough business to haul milk into town every day, sometimes re-maining in Tombstone overnight. Although the dairy was making good money, Alice was unhappy. She had never been a strong woman and the loss of her friends and the comforts of living in a town were a hardship to her. Life on a ranch in the desert meant hauling water, gathering firewood, and living with the threat of an Apache attack. The young woman and her two daughters spent their time in constant fear — and with good cause.

Fierce Apache war parties roamed the territory where there were few military posts and not enough soldiers to defend the settlers. The land had belonged to the Indians for thousands of years, and they didn't plan to give it to the white men. The settlers, however, were a hardy group who were determined to live and prosper in the rich valleys of southern Arizona. Their families endured the constant threat of attack, the often-deadly heat and the loneliness that is part of life in the desert.

The majority of the settlers built their homes to withstand an Indian attack. They always kept a large supply of guns and ammunition that even the smallest child in the family usually knew how to handle. The Apaches were known to sneak silently up to a house, and then fill the air with bloodcurdling war cries as they rushed in to capture the inhabitants. Most of the time the settlers managed to hold their own. When the warriors knew they couldn't succeed, they would pull back, wait for someone to try and escape, and then ambush the victim. Sometimes the families were lucky; the sound of gunshots were often heard by passing soldiers, and a troop would ride to the rescue.

As Alice heard stories of the horrible attacks, her terror of Apaches became so great that she and her girls thought every cactus looked like an Indian. Many times while Chris was away, they wouldn't cook or light the fire for fear the scent of food or smoke would attract a passing band of warriors. One night Chris arrived home and found his wife and daughters huddled behind the stove — Alice was so nervous she was becoming ill.

The harsh life of the desert and the fear of Apaches were so hard on Alice that the family moved back to Tombstone. They settled in a house with a yard large enough to keep their cattle, and the dairy business continued to flourish. Ethel was able to attend school for a brief time before her father purchased property at Waterville, about three miles outside of Tombstone.

While living at Waterville, the two young girls walked the long way to school each morning and hurried home in the afternoon. The reason for haste was the dust created by a drought. The ore teams returning from the mills churned thick clouds that invaded their nose and throats and covered their clothes from head to toe. Since there was barely enough water to drink, washing was almost impossible. The drought was so bad that the cattle were dying, so Chris again moved the family back to town. Once more Alice had to pack their things and load the wagon. The year was 1887, and she was about to give birth to another daughter, Olive.

When they reached Tombstone, the Robertsons moved across the street from the family of John Slaughter, who was the sheriff of Cochise County. Slaughter had the reputation of never bringing any man back "alive," but he was kind to the children and the families became close friends. Mrs. Slaughter was always on hand to help Alice, who was in very poor health. The young woman had developed a severe cough that never seemed to get better, and she could barely care for her family. By that time Ethel was used to remaining at home to help her mother, attending school whenever she could find time. During the next few years her assistance became very valuable. Alice gave birth to two more children, Curtis and George; she was very ill.

The Slaughters were caring people who knew Ethel rarely had any time to enjoy outside activities; she was becoming a woman long before her time. When they invited her to go with them on a vacation, Alice, to everyone's surprise, let the girl go. Although she was frail and needed her daughter, Alice did not want to deny Ethel a vacation.

Those few weeks were one of the happiest periods in the girl's life. There was someone else to cook and clean and no crying babies. She ran freely with the other young people and had a wonderful time. Unfortunately, it did not last. Ethel's father sent word to her that she would have to return home immediately — she was needed. Never again in her life would Ethel be so happy and carefree; responsibility would hold her back the rest of her youth.

When Ethel arrived home she was shocked to see how ill her mother had become. Like all children, Ethel thought her mother would live forever. Alice had what was called "quick consumption," and she was expecting her eighth child. The doctor was afraid that neither the mother nor her child would survive, and he was right. Before Alice passed on she made Ethel promise to keep her brothers and sisters together. With her mother's weak hand held tightly in her own strong one, the girl, who was just 14, accepted the burden of raising her siblings. The rigors of giving birth to so many children, as well as the hardships Alice had endured, finally took their toll — at the time of her death the once happy, young bride was only 31 years old, and her husband was so grief stricken he couldn't cope.

ETHEL

With her mother's death, Ethel had to assume the care of her four younger brothers and sisters. Although she was devastated over the loss of the gentle woman who had always been there to guide her, the young girl had no one to turn to in her grief. Shortly after the funeral, her father left his family to work in Pearce, a new mining town 16 miles from Tombstone.

Although the children were accustomed to being with their older sister, they were also used to having their mother's love. With her gone from their lives the young Robertsons needed comfort as well as care. Ethel found she could soothe them by reading stories. Some nights, however, that simply wasn't enough. At those times, she would take pillows, blankets, and the children to the home of one of their neighbors where they would all sleep on the floor. The knowledge that they were with adults seemed to make everyone feel better, including Ethel.

When Chris finally realized he had to make better arrangements for his children, he hired a family to live in his home and take over their care. This allowed Ethel and her younger sister Edith a chance to return to school. A year later Chris established a general store and livery stable in Pearce, and the business prospered. He was so successful that Ethel was able to start a preparatory class at the new University of Arizona, something the girl had never dreamed possible. As she boarded the train at Cochise along with the other students, her spirits rose; it was the first time she had ever been on her own.

At the University Ethel found she was a bright student and able to learn quickly. A new life opened up for the young woman who made friends easily. But once again fate stepped in. Her father's letters expressed his unhappiness. Things were not going well and he felt she should be in Tombstone where she was needed. Thanksgiving week Ethel received word from him that she had to come back home to stay; he could not manage without her. Ethel looked around at her friends and the school she so enjoyed, and with a heavy heart she put those happy days behind her and returned to Tombstone.

When Ethel was 18, tragedy again struck the little family. There were many train robberies that year, and her father was a witness to one of them. The gunmen, fearing they had been recognized, sent 19-year-old Sid Page to "take care" of Chris Robertson. The man found Chris and shot him to death in cold blood. When he was arrested, Page claimed it was self-defense, but Chris was not even carrying a gun.

The children were playing nearby and heard the shots, but they didn't realize their father had been killed. Ethel was at home when one of her friends rushed in to tell her the heartbreaking news. At first she was too stunned to talk. Her family had already endured so much pain, and now this! As her friend put her arms around Ethel she heard her say, "Oh God, give me strength!" The friend held her tight and advised her to "live each day, just one day at a time. It will not be easy, but you will make it." Those words gave Ethel the ability to survive the years ahead. Whenever things got bad, she would say to herself, "I will just take one day at a time, and until we are hungry I won't worry." And, they never did go hungry.

In December, Sid Page's case went to Court. Edith was 14 at the time, so she and Ethel went to his trial together. When they saw their father's bloody clothing as evidence, both girls averted their eyes; it was just too terrible to endure.

Feelings were high in the courtroom, but the people kept their anger to themselves. Chris was a popular man who was not known to have hurt anyone. In those days, everybody was afraid to speak out, for Tombstone was a violent town. When the jury reached a guilty verdict, Sid Page was sentenced to life in prison. The girls left the courthouse feeling his fate was in the hands of the Lord; they did not hate the young man, but only felt pity for him.

Chris had died without leaving a will. At the time of his death he was worth over $70,000, most of it in property. Since all of his children were minors, they were made wards of the court. The estate, however, was going to buy them a place of their own, and with a little luck they found a spacious old house with a large yard. But the home had one problem — it came with a court appointed guardian who was paid $75 a month. Ethel was to receive the same amount for the support of herself and her four siblings.

Unfortunatley, when the family moved, the guardian, a course, overbearing man, went with them. Ethel was as capable as any adult, and something was bound to happen; it did. One day the guardian went too far when he slapped one of her little brothers. This was totally unacceptable. Ethel grabbed him by his dirty whiskers and literally threw the uninvited man out of the house. When she realized what she had done, the girl sat down and cried. Ethel knew she had stepped over the line by breaking the rules. And that is how her neighbor found the young woman, sitting on the porch with tears streaming down her cheeks. The neighbor, who was a very kind and prominent citizen, said she knew what had been happening and would accompany Ethel to court.

When the very frightened Ethel and her neighbor arrived for the hearing, the lady waved her umbrella at the curious onlookers and said, "Get out of here you old carrion crows," and they fled. The judge was aware of the family's troubles, and after hearing what happened he appointed another guardian. This man was entirely different from his predecessor. He blended in with the children who found him helpful as well as kind when asked for advice. Despite her fears, Ethel was able to keep her promise to her mother; the children were to remain together.

Ethel realized she couldn't support the family on $75 a month, so she and Edith went to work at the Cochise County Courthouse recording the tax rolls. At that time clerks had to have excellent penmanship and both girls easily qualified. They were the first women to be employed by the County. Their salary from the courthouse, with the $75 they received from the estate, allowed them to maintain the standard of living that Ethel knew her parents would have wanted.

When she reached 21, Ethel petitioned the court for custody of the children. Although her father had been dead only three years, the court-appointed officials had completely depleted his estate and it seemed Ethel owed them $400! She said she would accept full responsibility of caring for her brothers and sisters, but she would not pay the court one penny — and she never did.

With that behind her, Ethel relaxed. Her love of all children became apparent to everyone when she began taking in young boarders. Many of the children went to school in Tombstone, and stayed with Ethel and her family while their parents lived and worked at various mining camps around the town. The care of youngsters and their rights became a cause that remained with Ethel the rest of her life. She soon gained the reputation as a guardian of children in need and would cheerfully provide a good meal, warm bed, and friendship to any waif who appeared at her door.

One little schoolmate of her youngest sister, Olive, came to spend the night and remained for 14 years. The child, whose name was Sadie, had lost her mother, and her father's job at the mine kept him from spending time with his daughter. Since Olive needed someone close to her age, Sadie stayed on and they became life-long friends. With the addition of Sadie, the Robertson family grew a bit larger.

By the time Ethel was 22, the whole family worked as a team. She provided their religious training and instructed them to avoid the red-light districts where all the problems were, just as her mother had taught her so many years ago.

Edith was the first one to break the family circle when she married and moved away. Right after that, a crew of top engineers was brought in to sink the boom shaft of the Grand Central Mine. The foreman was James Herbert "Bert" Macia, and he fell in love with the charming Miss Robertson. When his crew moved on, Bert remained. After a whirlwind courtship, Ethel found she also loved him. They were soon married and left on a brief honeymoon. When the newlyweds returned, it was to their ready-made family of Olive, George, Curtis, and Sadie.

During the next few years, Ethel and Bert worked hard to provide the growing family with an education as well as a background of faith and love. From the start of their marriage, the Macia's home became headquarters for young people and it remained that way. Ethel had always been an active member of the Episcopal Church, and Tombstone was a very social place. There were teas, dances, and other activities that were part of "church life" and the family always attended them together.

In 1908, Ethel and Bert were blessed with a daughter, Iris, and the young Robertsons were beginning to find their wings and leave the nest. When the water problems of 1911 caused the mines to close, many families moved on, but the Macias remained. Bert tried ranching, but he wasn't happy, for mining was in his blood. At that time Tombstone depended almost entirely on the County Courthouse and the business it created. Since there were few jobs available, Bert created his own business. He began operating mines throughout the southwest, always maintaining headquarters in his own town. Ethel continued caring for children, and in 1914, she had another daughter, Jeanne. A year and a half later a son completed the Macia family. Ethel had no desire to have as many children as her poor mother. Her love and sad memories of that overworked, fragile woman would always be close to her heart.

With Bert gone most of the time, Ethel cared for her children and home, but she felt the need to expand and provide a secure income for the family. When the Arcade Hotel (formerly the Cochise House) went up for sale, the Macias purchased it. The old hotel had been in operation since the boom days of Tombstone, and Ethel found herself the proprietress of one of the town's favorite hotels. She began serving the meals family style on large tables, and her guests were numbered among the elite of Tombstone's society. The Macia youngsters were usually on hand to help their mother provide the comfortable atmosphere of dining at home. Their new venture was successful.

When Ethel and Bert purchased the hostelry, they also became the caretakers of a very special rose plant in their patio. She was named the Lady Banksia and had arrived as a cutting from England in 1885. The "Lady" was a gift to a young bride from Scotland who in turn gave some shoots to the landlady of the Arcade Hotel. Although the rose was planted, it never really thrived until the Macias moved into their new lodging. The minute Ethel saw the little rose struggling for survival in the dry, arid soil of southern Arizona, her nurturing instincts took over. As she watered the Lady and talked to her, Ethel became fond of the strange plant, and the rose showed her appreciation by springing to life with astonishing new growth. The patio became Ethel's special place to relax, as she sat beside the Lady Banksia.

Although she was busy, Ethel continued to take in needy children and she eventually became involved in bringing together people who had the means to start a children's home in Arizona. Unfortunately, she was not successful; costs were high and no one could decide where to build it. Later, Ethel served as the southeastern Arizona representative on the executive board of the Arizona Children's Home in Tucson. She also conducted their annual fund-raiser.

When the citizens of Cochise County voted to move the County Seat from Tombstone to Bisbee, the town began to wither, but it was still too tough to die. During that time the only meals served were at the Arcade Hotel. Since Tombstone had a large Mexican population, Ethel attempted to provide them with jobs as well as food and clothing.

Meanwhile, the Lady Banksia had become a ferocious climber, and would attach herself to whatever was handy. Bert tried to cut the plant back, or tie it up, but nothing worked, for it had grown into a tree. He finally built a wooden trellis to train the Lady, but she soon outgrew even that. As the tree continued to climb upward and outward she attracted worldwide attention. In 1937, Robert Ripley, the famed creator of *Ripley's Believe It or Not,* declared it was "The World's Largest Rose Tree." Inevitably, the hotel and the tree became synonymous, and in 1939, the Arcade Hotel became the Rose Tree Inn.

As the Macia children began to start lives of their own, Ethel became interested in the romantic history of her colorful state. Her next few years were spent gathering material and data throughout Arizona. She kept meticulous records and factual information, which grew into an outstanding library. Her collection became an important source of knowledge for many authors of the day. Ethel later became historian of the Arizona State Federation of Women's Clubs.

In 1941, the Macias sold the Inn to their daughter and son-in-law, Jeanne and Burt Devere. However, they both continued to live there the rest of their lives.

When World War II broke out, the Rose Tree Inn became a "home front" to the locals and a hub of activity with everyone in the family working for the war effort. The lobby of the Inn became a favorite meeting place for the ladies to gather together and knit millions of mittens, socks, and scarves for the armed services. The Macia's son, James, became a navigator/bombardier and was one of the volunteers to serve under Jimmy Doolittle in the famous 1942 Tokyo raid.

Everything was put on hold during that terrible period, except the Lady Banksia who continued to grow. Her massive branches reached out in all directions and Bert was kept busy digging holes for posts and pipes to hold her limbs. The tree eventually covered the entire patio, and when the war ended, tourists began flocking to the Inn to see the unbelievable tree.

Bert Macia passed away in 1951; he was a miner to the end. His assay office was given in its entirety to the Tombstone Restoration Commission, and eventually became part of the Old Cochise County Courthouse. Ethel bore the grief she felt over the loss of her husband by continuing to give to the living. She was in great demand as an historian and served in advisory capacity for the annual Helldorado Celebration. In 1953, she rode at the head of the parade as the "Queen of Helldorado," a fitting title for a great lady.

Jeanne and Burt Devere closed the Rose Tree Inn in 1954, making it their home. The patio, with its Lady, however, remained open to the public. Each year thousands of visitors flocked to marvel at the hundreds upon hundreds of delicate white rose blossoms that covered the tree every April. It was during that time Ethel loved to sit by her rose and entertain tourists with the fascinating history of Arizona.

The National Broadcasting Company staged its television program, *Wide, Wide, World*, in 1955, from Tombstone. It was a nationwide, live show with no taping. There were Apache villages, Indian pole dances, and a reenactment of historical events by the Vigilantes. Ethel Macia was chosen to narrate the event. On the day of the broadcast, she sat in Boothill Cemetery as composed and beautiful as any movie star, and never missed a director's cue. Whether she was speaking to one person or a million who were unseen, history was history to Ethel and she was a master at presenting it.

Her elegance and composure in Ethel's one and only TV appearance earned her the title of "The First Lady of Tombstone," a name she cherished. Following that, Ethel continued to live an active life in the town she knew and loved. In 1964, the Devere family reopened the old Inn as The Rose Tree Museum. Later that year Ethel Robertson Macia passed away at the age of 83; her mind was crystal clear to the end.

During Ethel's lifetime she endured, without complaint, the obligations and trials life dealt her, and left a legacy of dedication and love. Her memory lingers among the members of her family and in the pages of the history of that wild, turbulent state she so loved. At the Rose Tree Museum, the Lady Banksia continues to grow, spreading her branches and reaching for the Heavens as though to touch the face of the gentle lady who had once been her friend.

*At the age of 14, Ethel took over the responsibility of
raising her four younger siblings.*

Ethel appears happy in a fancy new hat. This photo was taken shortly before the death of her father changed her life.

The Robertson Family in 1899

At the age of 18, Ethel became the head of her family when her father passed away. In this photo, Ethel is in the top row (left) next to her sister Edith. In the front row are Olive, Curtis, and George.

The Lady Banksia in full bloom.

In later years, Ethel became very fond of the Lady Banksia.

Ethel Macia holding her first child.

Ethel Robertson Macia

"The First Lady of Tombstone"

Tombstone's First Lady Recalls
Days of Gunfights

"Ethel Macia, 'First Lady of the Town Too Tough to Die,' was here when the guns were going off.

"Born in Tombstone 78 years ago, Mrs. Macia has never lived anywhere else and doesn't intend to change now. A charming mentally alert woman, she thinks some TV programs haven't done right by her town.

"'Of course, the cowboys let off steam when they came here in the old days, she recalled, but most of them weren't bad fellows. They led hard lives . . . TV tends to distort Tombstone history. The town was in a bad shape with so many saloons and gambling halls. We were forbidden to go near Allen and 6th. That was the red-light district. One thing about the prostitutes in those days, they knew their place and stayed in it. They didn't parade on the street and mingle with respectable people. They paid a license fee to operate."

"Most of the prostitutes were French girls, many of them from Paris. We school kids called them the 6th Street Girls. Some of the girls were capable of good-hearted deeds and did kindly things. I remember when a little girl was severely burned and suffering horribly. That night one of the prostitutes came to the parents' home, to the back door, and said she had brought a lotion if the parents would accept it. It relieved the girl's suffering, but she died the next day.'"

— Excerpted from *Citizen News,* 1959

In 1880, the wild boomtown of Tombstone had 110 liquor licenses, many gambling establishments, and numerous brothels. It also was the home of the Bird Cage Theatre, which was called by the New York Times the bawdiest, most wicked honky tonk in America. The notorious theatre became the inspiration for the song, "She Was Only a Bird in a Gilded Cage," which aptly described the "ladies" who worked there.

Courtesy of The Rose Tree Museum

The Lady Banksia

The Lady Banksia

The Lady Banksia Rose, "The World's Largest Rose Tree," celebrated her 117th blooming season in April 2002. The Rose Tree is Tombstone's most famous "Shady Lady." She was planted in that town in 1885, and unlike the various gunfighters who stayed a short time and went on their way, she has remained, growing more beautiful with the passing years.

The "Town Too Tough To Die," was nearly done for in 1937, when Robert Ripley, of the famous Ripley's Believe It or Not *visited Tombstone. He gave the Lady Banksia Rose the title of The World's Largest Rose Tree, and to date it has never been disputed. The* Guinness' Book of World Records *also lists her as "The World's Largest Rose Tree." The unbelievable spread of branches and blooms are supported by pipes and posts that cover an area of over 8,000 square feet. The trunk is approximately 12 feet in circumference.*

How did this lovely lady come to be in Tombstone where the city populace was known for planting men, not rose bushes? It was a young Scottish woman, Mary Gee, who was responsible. Mary, the bride of a mining engineer who worked for the Old Guard Mining Company, was staying at the Cochise House while her own home was being built. She was homesick for her native Scotland and its green hills. Her family thought it would cheer her up to have some part of her homeland with her and they sent her several plants and cuttings, one of which was her favorite, the Lady Banksia Rose.

During the time Mary and Henry Gee resided at the Cochise House, Mary became great friends with the proprietress. When her plants arrived, Mary gave one of the Lady Banksia to her friend, and together they planted it in the back yard of the Cochise House. When Ethel and Bert Macia took over the ownership, Ethel nurtured the rose into the famous tree of today.

— Courtesy of The Rose Tree Museum

"It was common practice in the slave states for ladies, when angry with their maids, to send them to the calybuse [sic] sugarhouse, or to some other place established for the purpose of punishing slaves, and have them severely flogged; and I am sorry it is a fact, that the villains to whom those defenseless creatures are sent, not only flog them as they are ordered, but frequently compel them to submit to the greatest indignity.

"Oh! If there is any one thing under the wide canopy of heaven horrible enough to stir a man's soul, and to make his very blood boil, it is the thought of his dear wife, his unprotected sister, or his young and virtuous daughter struggling to save themselves from falling prey to such demons!"

William Craft, 1860
London, England

Chapter 4

ELLEN CRAFT
A RACE FOR FREEDOM

Although Ellen Craft was not part of the history of the early West, her compelling story of courage in the face of overwhelming odds belongs with the stories of these other brave women.

The West is not just a geographical area, it is also a state of mind with a spirit of its own. Ellen shared this spirit as she fled from Georgia to Massachusetts as a slave in search of freedom.

Ellen was born in a small cabin in Clinton, Georgia, in about 1826. Her father, Major James Smith, one of the richest men in central Georgia, was the owner of a large plantation with nearly one hundred, hardworking slaves; Ellen's mother, Maria, was one of them. She had been purchased while still a child and, because of her light complexion, became one of the many "house wenches."

As a house servant, Maria was allowed to wear her mistress's cast-off clothing and eat the leftover scraps from the table. She learned the ways of the house and had the privilege of living in her own small cabin. It was that small cabin the Major began to visit late at night shortly after Maria turned 14. Since she was just a slave, Maria legally belonged to her master and could not defend herself. Her daughter, Ellen, was born about a year later — and the night visits stopped.

Unfortunately, the child arrived a year after Mrs. Smith, the Major's wife, had her fifth child. The resemblance between the two children was so great visitors often thought Ellen was part of the Major's legitimate family, not the daughter of his slave.

Ellen was a pretty little girl with white skin, straight black hair, and beautiful dark eyes. Although the Major was known for being a kind man, he never acknowledged Ellen as his daughter. There were other white men in the South, however, who did recognize their illegitimate children.

As she grew older, the resemblance between Ellen and the Major's legal children became so pronounced that visiting gentlemen often complimented Mrs. Smith for her beautiful family. Many claimed the little girl, in particular, looked just like the Major. The continuous praise of Ellen, who Mrs. Smith referred to as a worthless "yard-child," began to anger the good lady. When the gentlemen left, she would order the innocent girl to the barn for punishment, which came in the form of terrible beatings.

Maria loved her daughter, but wasn't able to protect her from the constant abuse. She knew the Major would not lift a finger to help. Ellen learned to bear her painful treatment stoically, for she was a strong-willed child — it was that strength that would serve her through the years ahead.

By the time Ellen reached 11, Mrs. Smith could hardly bear the sight of the unwanted child; she was a constant reminder of one of her husband's many infidelities. One day the distraught woman found a way to rid herself of the girl. Her oldest daughter was marrying a man from Macon, Georgia; she would give Ellen to her as a wedding gift to serve as a personal maid. Maria was devastated when her daughter was taken away from her, and Ellen was filled with both pain and anger. She wondered how she could be given away like a set of china.

Ellen's life improved after she left Mrs. Smith, but she missed her mother so much that her heart ached constantly. Although her new mistress was not cruel, she never showed any affection for the little girl who was her half-sister. All the woman requested of Ellen was that she do her work and stay out of sight.

In her new home Ellen assumed the duties of a lady's maid. She helped her mistress dress and comb her hair and eventually began to sew a few of her garments. Ellen enjoyed sewing so much she soon became an excellent seamstress and began creating beautiful gowns. Her mistress was so pleased she allowed Ellen to live in a small cabin where she could also keep her sewing materials. Unlike her mother, Ellen was not forced to entertain a night visitor; her new master was far too old to be interested in a young slave girl.

As Ellen grew into a young woman she began making friends with the other workers, occasionally attending an unsupervised party. At one of these gatherings she met William Craft, a cabinetmaker from another plantation. In Georgia, a slave who was skillful at his trade was provided a pass and allowed to work outside for a businessman in the city; William was one of those slaves. Although all of his wages went to his owner, William managed to save money for himself by doing jobs for others and working long, extra hours.

It was natural for Ellen and William's friendship to grow as they had many things in common. She had been taken from her mother, and William watched as his elderly parents and siblings were sold one by one at auction. When William was 16, he and his 14-year-old sister, Sarah, were the only members of his family belonging to the same owner. When the owner lost his money they were both sold.

William watched as his sister was taken with the others to be auctioned off like cattle, and then dragged away by a new master. As the cart carrying Sarah rolled down the road, she turned to her brother for help, but he wasn't even allowed to say good-bye. William knew he was just chattel, with no legal rights, and he was filled with hatred. That tight knot of hatred began to dissolve when he met Ellen. She was so small and defenseless that the 23-year-old man wanted only to protect her from harm.

The friendship of Ellen and William developed into love, but she constantly refused to marry him. Ellen had endured so much pain with the separation from her mother that she was reluctant to become attached to anyone again. The young woman couldn't bear the thought of losing William or any child they might have. She also realized her mistress could sell her at any time; a light female slave always brought a very high price.

After nearly a year, William convinced Ellen to marry him by promising they would find a way to escape. With the consent of their owners the couple was wed in the slave quarters — the marriage was not recognized by law, and the words "until death do us part" were omitted. Ellen added her own silent vow; she would bear no child until she was free.

Following the wedding William was allowed to share Ellen's small cabin, where they created a loving home of their own. For the next two years they spent many hours planning an escape. William figured they would have to travel at least 1,000 miles across the heart of the slave states in order to be free, a task that would not be simple. He knew slaveholders often traveled with a servant and that provided a glimmer of hope. Ellen was almost white, and if she could disguise herself as an invalid gentleman, William would travel with her as a faithful servant. In that way they might be able to reach freedom in the North.

When William first suggested the plan to his wife she shrank from the idea, claiming it was impossible. But the more she thought about their helpless situation, the more anxious she was to escape from it. After weeks of prayer, Ellen finally told William she thought the Lord was on their side and with His assistance she felt they would succeed.

With her words of encouragement William set out to gather the necessary items for his wife's disguise. Although he had saved a considerable amount of money over the years, it was almost impossible for a slave to buy anything without the consent of his master. William had to shop carefully, purchasing things piece by piece in different parts of the city.

Ellen worked at night attempting to create a fashionable suit befitting a young gentleman of wealth. Since she was beardless, Ellen devised a large bandage that resembled a poultice like those worn for an aching tooth. This would cover the lower part of her face and also deter any unnecessary conversation while traveling.

The couple planned to leave around the Christmas holidays. The more lenient owners would often give their favored slaves a few days off during that period so they could visit relatives. The Crafts needed written permission in case they were stopped. It took a lot of perseverance to get approval, but they finally received passes on the condition they return in seven days.

It was necessary for people traveling to register their name at the custom houses and hotels along the way. The couple decided Ellen would assume the name of Mr. William Johnson, a wealthy plantation owner. Then a terrible thought occurred to Ellen, one so obvious that she couldn't understand why they hadn't considered it before; she couldn't write her name. Few slaves were allowed the privilege of reading or writing, and any owner in Georgia caught educating his people was severely punished.

The couple was filled with a deep despair and felt that all their plans were worthless, but then Ellen had an idea. They would put her right arm in a sling as though it was broken and ask the officer in charge to sign for her. She also decided to add a limp in order to appear totally dependent upon her servant.

On December 18, it was time for them to leave. William cut his wife's hair short, placed a man's hat upon her head, and added a pair of green spectacles to hide any fear that might show in her eyes. Ellen resembled a proper, very ill gentleman. They safely tucked their passes away, knelt together in prayer, and embraced. Both knew any form of affection would be impossible until they reached their destination. Then, with faith in their hearts, the Crafts silently slipped out of their cabin just before dawn.

They took different routes to the railroad station to avoid being seen together. From then on Ellen knew the success or failure of their escape depended upon her.

She arrived first with the majority of passengers, purchased tickets for herself and her servant to Savannah, and paid to have her luggage put aboard. William arrived just before the train was to leave, hid his face, and jumped into the car carrying the other colored people. The first lap of their long journey was about to begin — as the train pulled away, neither of the Crafts looked back.

Ellen chose a window seat to keep from being recognized. Just as she began to relax, a man sat down beside her and, to her dismay, she discovered he was an old friend of her master. In fact, he had known Ellen since she was a girl. When he attempted to start a conversation, she ignored him by looking out the window. He said, "Isn't it a fine day, sir?" She didn't reply for fear he would recognize her voice. Then he repeated his question in a louder tone, and when there was still no answer, he yelled the same question. Before Ellen could respond, another passenger quietly said, "It is a terrible thing to be deaf!" The man sitting next to her said no more.

With her first hurdle behind, Ellen, who had been holding her breath, found she could breathe again. During the rest of the trip the conversation that flowed around her was mostly about blacks, cotton, and the "damned abolitionists." Ellen had always heard that abolitionists were evil men, and she was delighted to learn they were kind people who were opposed to slavery.

When the train arrived in Savannah, the Crafts rode a coach to the docks where the steamer bound for Charleston, South Carolina, was waiting. As soon as they boarded Ellen excused herself and went to her cabin, for she was exhausted. The other passengers questioned William about his young master and wondered why he had retired so early. William explained that the poor man suffered from painful rheumatism, and was on his way North to receive better medical treatment. Then he went off to find a place to spend the rest of the trip, only to find there were no provisions for colored passengers, whether they were slaves or free men. William spent the rest of the day walking around the decks and slept on a bale of cotton during the night.

In the morning William went to help his wife with her disguise and escorted her carefully to a seat at the breakfast table. The captain, who had been observing William's attentiveness, remarked to Ellen that she had a good "boy." Then he warned her to watch him carefully because the abolitionists were always ready to steal a valuable servant. Before she could reply, a rough looking slave-dealer nodded his head in agreement and said, "Sound doctrine captain, very sound. I would never take a black North . . . if you make up your mind to sell him, I am your man!" The suggestion was so distasteful that Ellen put her fork down and in a strong voice informed the obnoxious dealer she could not get along without her servant. Then she limped away from the table.

As the steamer neared Charleston, Ellen thanked the captain for his courtesy and hobbled onto the deck. There she was engaged in conversation by a young southern military officer who was also traveling with a man servant. He gently accused her of spoiling her boy with kindness and told her she should keep him shaking with fear so he would remain in his place and be humble. With those words, the officer shook Ellen's hand and walked away.

The Crafts left the steamer at Charleston, and took a carriage to the depot where they were to board a train for Richmond, Virginia. When they arrived at Customs, Ellen requested a ticket for both of them as she had done before, but this time the officer appeared suspicious. He glared at William and yelled, "Boy do you belong to this gentleman?" When William said, "Yes sir," the officer handed Ellen the tickets and asked her to sign her name and that of her boy in the register and then pay a dollar duty on him.

She paid the dollar without a hint of the fear she felt, pointed to her arm in its sling, and requested the officer to sign for her. This infuriated the man and he refused. A large group of curious people had gathered to see what was happening. When Ellen looked at the strange faces that surrounded her, she must have realized she and William were all alone in the heart of the South with no friend or relative who could help them. Just as she was about to panic, the military officer who had spoken to her the day before stepped forward and came to her rescue. He appeared to have consumed a large amount of alcoholic beverages and was in a generous mood. The officer even spoke to William as though they had known each other for years. When the trainmaster saw to whom Ellen was talking, he went up to her and offered to accept the responsibility. She said her name was Mr. William Johnson and he signed the register. Later, the Crafts wondered how both the southern officer and the trainmaster felt when the news of their escape was published.

When they boarded the train Ellen was so tired that all she wanted to do was find a place to sit. Her limp caught the attention of an elderly gentleman in the company of his two unmarried daughters, and he asked William about the young man's illness. When he received the usual answer, he was kind enough to invite the poor invalid to travel with his family. Ellen was practically forced into the seat next to them and requested to lie down and rest. She was too tired to complain and the daughters gently placed their shawls around her. They whispered to their father that they thought "he" was a very nice young man.

Unfortunately, the young girls seemed to have been attracted to the wrong "man." When they left the train, the father handed Ellen his card and urged him to visit his plantation. Mr. Johnson expressed his gratitude for their help, and then without looking at the card for fear they would discover she couldn't read, Ellen quickly put it in her pocket.

On Christmas Eve they reached Baltimore, Maryland, the last stop before the free states. William again helped his wife on the train, and then went off to join the other slaves; he too was exhausted. As he started to climb into the baggage car, a conductor grabbed William by the shoulder and asked where he was going. When William answered Philadelphia, he was almost yanked off the train. The conductor appeared to be in a bad mood and yelled at William to quickly find his master! It was against the rules to allow a black man any further north unless his master could show documents of ownership.

Ellen had just taken her seat when William appeared with the bad news. She took one look at her husband and saw the terrible look of fear and defeat in his eyes, and became furious. They had been through so much and now this. Whatever was to happen in the next few minutes depended entirely upon her. She took a deep breath, squared her shoulders under their male attire, and hurried to face the stationmaster.

In a strong voice Ellen said, "Do you want to see me?" He replied in an insulting manner that he could not allow any black out of

Baltimore without proof of ownership. Although Ellen knew this was impossible for her to do, she never faltered. She had lived all of her life among the upper class Southerners who knew how to treat their underlings, and she felt qualified to handle this one. In her most imperious tone she answered, "I bought tickets in Charleston to pass us on through to Philadelphia, you have no right to detain us." To that, he replied that right or wrong he wasn't going to let them through. These sharp words were like the crack of doom to the Crafts who felt they were caught in a trap.

The other passengers had been listening to the conversation and all were watching Mr. Johnson. Just to hear him speak anyone would know he was a gentleman, and also very ill. While Ellen stood there waiting, she never took her eyes off the stationmaster who had the power to destroy her future. Her challenging stare made the man uncomfortable and the passengers began to side with Mr. Johnson, demanding that he and his slave be allowed to travel on.

When the final bell rang the people aboard the train, the stationmaster dropped his eyes and told the conductor to let them both pass through. Ellen thanked him brusquely, as though she had received what was due, and, taking William's arm, she hobbled across the platform. He gently helped her to her seat and the train departed with a puff of steam. In nine hours they would be in Philadelphia; Ellen stayed awake all night watching the lights go by.

The train arrived in Philadelphia just before dawn and William was there to assist her into a carriage. In his many conversations with the other colored people riding in the Jim Crow cars, William had acquired the name of a boarding house owned by abolitionists. He knew they would be safe there. As the carriage pulled away, Ellen burst into tears — it was Christmas Day, 1848, and they had received the greatest gift of all — freedom. . . .

While Ellen had carried off the role of Mr. Johnson, she kept wonderfully calm, successfully hiding her fears. Now that she was on free soil she broke down, tearfully asking William over and over again to reassure her they were safe. When they arrived at the boarding house she was so weak there was no further need to act as an invalid, for she had become one.

William arranged for lodging and gently helped his wife to their room; as soon as the door was closed they both dropped to their knees to thank God for helping them to safety. After a few hours rest, Ellen threw the hated disguise away and dressed in her own clothing. Then the couple went into the parlor to talk to the proprietor. When the man saw a charming woman instead of a young man he was astonished and eager to hear their story.

After William described their daring escape, the landlord praised their courage and sent a messenger to invite a few of the abolitionists to join them. Friends soon arrived to welcome the Crafts and congratulated the couple for their miraculous journey. As much as they wanted to help, they advised William not to remain in Philadelphia as planned. It was too close to the slave states. Instead, they suggested the Crafts move on to Boston as soon as Ellen regained her strength.

Arrangements were made for Ellen and William to be taken to the farm of a Quaker family just outside the city. It was this kind, affectionate family who taught Ellen that not all white people were cruel. While there, the Crafts learned part of the alphabet and to sign their names legibly. When it was time to leave for Boston, Ellen and William felt they were parting from relatives.

When the couple reached Boston they found a home ready for them. As soon as they were able, the Crafts asked to be married in the eyes of the law. The ceremony took place at the home of a respected Boston family, with the Reverend Parker officiating; this time the words "until death do us part" were included.

William had no trouble finding employment as a cabinetmaker, and Ellen opened a small dressmaking shop. Although both suspected their former owners were looking for them, they felt entirely safe in Boston, where they were making new friends. One of those friends was William Brown, a self-educated ex-slave who had successfully escaped 15 years earlier. Brown was in Boston lecturing against slavery and was well known for his work in human rights. He encouraged William and Ellen to attend anti-slavery meetings, and they soon became involved in the "cause." The Crafts eventually began making public appearances in several cities. They described the pain of being owned by another person and told of their own desperate escape. Ellen was extremely popular with the northern women, for few had ever met a female who had been a slave.

In 1850, Congress passed the Fugitive Slave Bill, and the Crafts' dreams of freedom were shattered. The bill declared the inhabitants of the free states would receive heavy penalties if they provided food and shelter to any hunted human being. It also said the people should assist, if called upon by the authorities, to seize the fugitives and send them back to their masters for punishment.

The Crafts did not want to make trouble for their friends, yet they were terrified of being returned to slavery. William had heard their owners had warrants for their arrests, and agents were already in Boston to pick them up. He felt helpless and knew there were two choices open to them: he and Ellen could remain in Boston and fight for their freedom or join the mass exodus of terrified slaves struggling to get to Canada, a country that did not want them. It would be impossible to leave by sea for officers were watching all the ports. William's friends advised him to take the expensive overland route to Halifax, Nova Scotia, and travel on to England, where they would be welcome.

At first William refused to leave his home and new life where he was happy and productive. He claimed he would rather die fighting. Ellen, however, knew they had to leave, and in time William reluctantly agreed. They would both have to act as normal as possible while waiting for arrangements to be made by their friends and the Underground Railroad. During that time Ellen gave the impression of being calm, just as she had during their flight from Georgia. She continued with her dressmaking and smiled at her customers, while inwardly shaking with fear.

When the time came to leave Boston, Ellen was separated from William and taken out of the city to stay with people who were well known for their kindness to oppressed slaves. She remained with them several days while waiting for her husband. When William finally arrived he quickly embraced his wife and told her they must leave at once. There was no time to spare, for every moment they spent at the home of those good people, the more trouble they caused them. The Crafts left in a hurry under cover of darkness — this time William carried a gun.

The journey through Canada was difficult. Many of the Canadian people they met were unfriendly toward people of color. Although they didn't threaten bodily harm, they were unpleasant and many times refused the couple food and lodging.

When the Crafts finally reached Halifax, they were provided with papers of introduction, given money, and then helped aboard a steamer leaving for England. The Crafts were once again running from slavery, hatred, and physical harm. As the ship pulled away from the dock, they both wondered what was ahead and if they would be welcome in England.

Their fears were, however, unnecessary. When the ship docked at Liverpool, Ellen and William were warmly received by friends of the abolitionists in Boston, and taken to London, where they were provided comfortable lodgings. Although many former slaves were able to flee to England, few were as successful as the Crafts. Their personal appearance was a great help. A reporter for *Chamber's Edinburgh Journal* described Ellen as "a gentle, refined looking creature of twenty-five years, as fair as most of her British sisters." He went on to write that William "was very dark, but of a reflective intelligent countenance, and of manly and dignified deportment."

The color of William's skin did not disturb the people of Great Britain as it had the Americans. Within a few months the Crafts became a highly respected, sought-after couple. Their new friends contributed funds for the education the Crafts had been denied in their own country. Ellen and William attended Ockham, a trade school for rural people founded by Lady Noel Byron, wife of the poet. The couple excelled in all subjects, and were soon teaching classes of their own. When their education had been completed, the school wanted the Crafts to stay as teachers, but both declined.

After leaving Ockham, William was offered a position with a group of businessmen to travel to Africa and set up trade in the region. Although Africa was a long way from England, William accepted the responsibility. He managed the business so competently that he traveled many times to Africa, becoming a respected merchant.

While her husband traveled, Ellen remained in London and continued to lecture. She earned a place in London's political and social life, and eventually founded a ladies' auxiliary to further help the plight of her people. Along with her new popularity, Ellen gained a sense of security and was no longer afraid to speak out and express her opinions.

In 1860, William wrote the book *Running a Thousand Miles to Freedom*, which was published in London. Thousands of copies of the book were sold throughout the world and other people learned of the injustice taking place in America.

The Crafts lived a successful, fulfilled life until 1868, when William decided they should return to America. He had heard the South had become a land of opportunity, with a need for experienced people. William's dream was to set up a cooperative in Georgia to help freed slaves. Before leaving England he managed to raise enough money for his venture, and, in 1869, the Crafts sailed for America, along with their five children, who had been born on the free soil of England — the Crafts had been in exile for almost 20 years.

Their first cooperative was in Georgia, near their former owners. Although the endeavor was a success, it was burned to the ground by nightriders who could not accept the fact that black people could prosper.

Ellen and William did not give up. They leased a run-down plantation named Woodville, near Savannah, and took on tenant farmers. William supplied the tools and seeds in exchange for a share of the crops, and everyone went to work. William left the plantation in his wife's hands while he went in search of funding. In his absence, Ellen and the farmers cleared the land, planted cotton and repaired the buildings. She opened a school in her dining room where she taught the children as well as their parents. During the years Ellen spent at Woodville, she became very fond of the plantation; it was the only real home, in her own country, she had known.

All of her hard work, however, was in vain. When the end of the first year arrived and they settled their accounts, William found the plantation was almost broke. It seemed no one grew wealthy in the South during the 1870s, when the price of cotton was low and taxes high. As the Crafts' debts increased, William was accused of swindling his backers. When he sued for libel, he lost.

The Crafts continued to work the plantation and it continued to fail. In 1890, Ellen and William finally left their dreams behind and moved in with their daughter and her husband, Dr. William Crum, a physician and activist. Ellen Craft died a year later in 1891. She was buried, at her request, near her favorite tree on Woodville — the plantation she loved.

With his wife's passing, William lost the love of his life as well as his strength. Without her all his ventures failed. He unsuccessfully attempted to regain control of Woodville and continued working for human rights. William Craft finally gave up and returned to his daughter's home in Charleston, South Carolina, where he passed away in 1899. At the time of his death, William was almost penniless.

Excerpted from the book
Running a Thousand Miles for Freedom

Having heard while in Slavery that "God made of one blood all nations of men," and also that the American Declaration of Independence says, that "We hold these truths to be self-evident, that all men are created equal: that they are endowed by their Creator with certain inalienable rights; that among these, are life, liberty, and the pursuit of happiness"; we could not understand by what right we were held as "chattels." Therefore, we felt perfectly justified in undertaking the dangerous and exciting task of "running a thousand miles" in order to obtain those rights which are so vividly set forth in the Declaration.

I beg those who would know the particulars of our journey, to peruse these pages.

This book is not intended as a full history of the life of my wife, nor of myself; but merely as an account of our escape; together with other matter which I hope may be the means of creating in some minds a deeper abhorrence of the sinful and abominable practice of enslaving and brutifying our fellow-creatures.

Without stopping to write a long apology for offering this little volume to the public, I shall commence at once to pursue my simple story.

— W. Craft

Ellen Craft

Disguised as a young Southern gentleman.

William Craft

Georgia Journal and Messenger
Macon, Georgia, June 25, 1851
Letter from Dr. Robert Collins to
S. J. Hastings of the *Boston Post*

". . . Does it not appear obvious to you, sir, that every Southern slaveholder has a deep interest at stake, both in the recapture and recovery by law, of his fugitive slaves! Every slave who gains his freedom from the South, and by protection of the North, presents to his fellow slaves the temptation to follow in his footsteps, and find the same freedom . . . If we of the South considered slavery a moral, social, and political evil, it would be easy for us to lessen the numbers of our slaves, by a system of gradual emancipation which would comport more with our own interests, and humanity to them . . . We believe that free negroes of the South are in a far more desirable condition, than the free negroes and fugitive slaves in the North. We also believe that it is our privilege and right to determine when and how and who of our slaves, ought to be made freedman. . . ."

Dr. Collins wanted Ellen returned. He claimed she belonged to him and was part of the family, who missed her. If Ellen's escape was successful, other slaves would follow; therefore, she should and must be used as an example to any other who dared to attempt an escape. He maintained Ellen, had she tried, could have earned her freedom — but he did not say how. Now, if captured, she faced degradation and shame or even death.

FEDERAL UNION — November 5, 1850
Fugitive Slave Law Again

In Boston the greatest excitement prevails with regard to execution of this law.

Instead of the fugitives, the claimants were three times arrested, first on an action for slander, and then for attempting to kidnap — and held to bail in a sum so large that few strangers would be able to give the requisite bail of $30,000 each. And when the bail was given, they had to hurry into a vehicle at the very portals of the temple of justice, and fly from the fury of a mob excited against them by hand bills, denouncing them as villains . . . and describing their persons as felons — thus:

Slave Hunters In Boston! ! !

"Authentic information has been received of the arrival in this city of a slave catcher from Macon, Georgia, named William H. Hewes, or Hughes, but who entered his name at the United States Hotel as Wm. Hamilton of New York; a short roudyish [sic] looking fellow, five-feet two, thirty or forty years of age, sandy hair, red whiskers, black short teeth, chews and smokes."

"He said yesterday, 'I am the jailer at Macon, I catch negroes sometimes; I am here for William and Ellen Craft and no one else, and damn 'em, I will have them if I stay till eternity; and if there are not men enough in Massachusetts to take them, I will bring them from the South. It is not the niggars [sic] I care for — it is the principle of the thing.'"

"Also a companion of the above, named John Knight, a tall, lank, lean looking fellow, five-feet ten or eleven inches high, dark hair, about twenty-eight years old."

"Also a professional slave catcher, Alfred Beal, from Norfolk, a very stout, thick set, coarse looking man, about five feet nine inches high, sandy hair, red whiskers, upper teeth broken off, about forty five years of age, known to be on a genuine hunt."

"All citizens, and especially all keepers of hotel and boarding houses, are required to keep close watch upon them, and others known in town."

☞ MEN OF BOSTON! ! ☜
SHALL THESE VILLAINS REMAIN HERE?
☞ It is the principle of the thing! ☜

100 DOLLARS
REWARD!

Runaway from the subscriber on the 27th of July, my Black Woman, named

EMILY,

**Seventeen years of age, well grown, black color, has a whining voice. She took with her one dark calico and one blue and white dress, a red corded gingham bonnet; a white striped shawl and slippers. I will pay the above reward if taken near the Ohio river on the Kentucky side, or THREE HUNDRED DOLLARS, if taken in the State of Ohio, and delivered to me near Lewisburg, Mason County, Ky.   THO'S. H. WILLIAMS
August 4, 1853.**

Courtesy of the Ohio Historical Society

Emily - Runaway Slave

Broadside dated August 4, 1853, announcing a reward for the apprehension and return of a runaway slave named Emily who belonged to Thomas H. Williams from near Lewisburg, Mason County, Kentucky.

$150 REWARD.

RANAWAY from the subscriber, on the night of Monday the 11th July, a negro man named

about 30 years of age, 5 feet 6 or 7 inches high; of dark color; heavy in the chest; several of his jaw teeth out; and upon his body are several old marks of the whip, one of them straight down the back. He took with him a quantity of clothing, and several hats.

  A reward of $150 will be paid for his apprehension and security, if taken out of the State of Kentucky; $100 if taken in any county bordering on the Ohio river; $50 if taken in any of the interior counties except Fayette; or $20 if taken in the latter county.

  july 12-84-tf   B.L. BOSTON.

Tom - Runaway Slave
Advertisement dated July 12 (year unknown) announcing
a reward for the apprehension of a runaway slave
named Tom who belonged to B.L. Boston of
Fayette County, Kentucky.

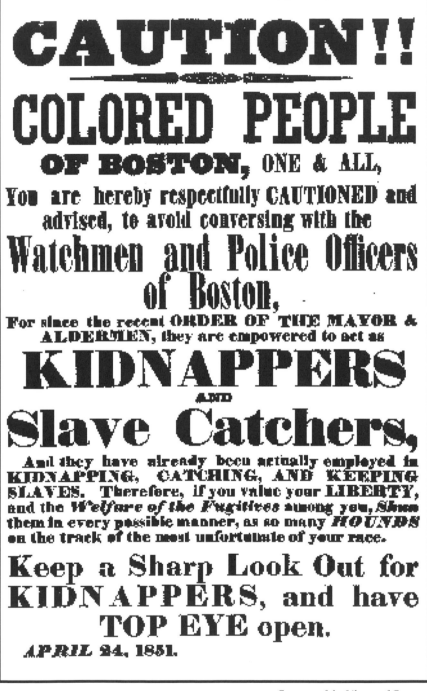

Courtesy of the Library of Congress

The Fugitive Slave Act 1850

Be it enacted by the Senate and House of Representatives of the United States of America in Congress assembled, That the persons who have been, or may hereafter be, appointed commissioners, in virtue of any act of Congress, by the Circuit Courts of the United States, and Who, in consequence of such appointment, are authorized to exercise the powers that any justice of the peace, or other magistrate of any of the United States, may exercise in respect to offenders for any crime or offense against the United States, by arresting, imprisoning, or bailing the same under and by the virtue of the thirty-third section of the act of the twenty-fourth of September seventeen hundred and eighty-nine, entitled "An Act to establish the judicial courts of the United States" shall be, and are hereby, authorized and required to exercise and discharge all the powers and duties conferred by this act.

In an attempt to appease the South, Congress passed the Compromise of 1850, which revised the Fugitive Slave Bill. The law gave slaveowners "the right to organize a posse at any point in the United States to aid in recapturing runaway slaves. Courts and police everywhere in the United States were obligated to assist them." Private citizens were also obligated to assist in the recapture of runaways. Furthermore, people who were caught helping slaves served jail time as well as paid fines and restitution to the slaveowner.

Courtesy of The Wyoming State Archives, Department of State Parks and Resources

Nellie Tayloe Ross

First woman governor of Wyoming

First woman governor in the United States

Chapter 5

NELLIE TAYLOE ROSS
THE FIRST LADY OF WYOMING

On November 7, 1924, the complacency of the male-dominated political arena was shattered when Nellie Tayloe Ross was elected by the people of Wyoming to serve as their first woman governor. Nellie neither sought the nomination nor campaigned. She was chosen by the Democratic Party to fulfill the seat left vacant by the death of her husband. Although Nellie only served two years, when she left office she was affectionately called "Our Nell" and known by many as a "cracking good governor."

Nellie Davis Tayloe was born on November 29, 1876, near St. Joseph, Missouri. She was the youngest child of John Tayloe, a well-to-do merchant by profession and gentleman farmer by avocation, and Elizabeth, a homemaker.

Nellie was not an extraordinary child in any way. She was a normal, happy little girl with deep-blue eyes and fly-away hair, who giggled when amused or embarrassed. If anyone would have claimed Nellie was destined to become the nation's first woman governor and the first woman director of the United States Mint, her two adoring older brothers might have died laughing — to them, the mere idea would have been preposterous.

When Nellie was old enough to begin her education, her father decided she should attend both public and private schools. Upon graduation from high school the young woman enrolled in a two-year course to become a teacher, and then taught kindergarten. At 25, Nellie had lost her childhood giggle and grown into a slender, attractive woman with a gentle Southern voice. She had many male admirers — none of whom interested her.

During a school break Nellie went for a visit to Paris, Tennessee, where she met William Bradford Ross, a man who would change her life forever. William was one of the state's most promising young attorneys, a sought-after orator and born politician. He was an extremely handsome man with the clean-cut good looks of a Western movie hero.

The couple was immediately attracted to each other and within a short time they were in love. In 1902, William married the only woman he would ever call sweetheart when the lovely Nellie Tayloe became his wife. The marriage was to be one of mutual respect and devotion.

Following their wedding the Rosses decided to leave Tennessee and move West. They hoped to carve out a successful career for William in the lively capital of Wyoming. By that time life in Cheyenne had calmed down. The city had outgrown its reputation of the 1880s when it was known as the "richest and toughest town on the continent." Although there were less shootings and fewer cowboys running their herds over unfenced ranges, the cattle barons were still plentiful. They lived quietly in gracious mansions amidst the splendor of their colorful past.

Life in Cheyenne was a constant source of delight and adventure for the young couple. They loved the magnificent mountains, clear clean air, and feeling of space that surrounded them. The Western people were friendly and the social life was exciting. It was a period of adjustment, parties, and new friends. The young attorney, however, soon became restless. He was eager to start his new law practice and his zest for politics was as strong as ever.

Since Nellie was a homemaker at heart, she too was ready to settle down and begin a family. Within a year they were expecting their first child. But when the twin boys, George and James, arrived, the parents realized they had their hands full. Both babies were small and sickly, and their exhausted mother spent many anxious days and nights watching over their frail little lives. She would have been overwhelmed with the care of one baby; two, however, were almost too much for the inexperienced young mother. In an interview with *Good Housekeeping Magazine*, Nellie said: "It was not often I surrendered to weakness, but I still remember one hour, and the distinct feeling that though those babies might survive the perils of infancy, their mother would never live to tell the tale."

Although William helped as much as he could with the ordeal of the twins, his law practice and political future were at stake. He was working hard to gain a name for himself within the Democratic Party, and in 1904, he achieved his first political success. William captured the seat in the Republican state to serve as court attorney. Although he won by a scant margin of 20 votes, it was still a victory.

The following year, Alfred, their third son arrived. Sadly, his was to be a short life for he passed away ten months later. The couple was devastated by their loss, but both knew life had to move forward. William buried his grief in his law practice and political advancement. Nellie was forced to put her sorrow behind to care for the active twins. The demise of her son had added a new dimension to her life — she had faced death. In later years Nellie often claimed it was a lesson that helped her prepare for the terrible tragedy that was to come.

Entertainment was almost non-existent for the Rosses. Motion pictures of that era were not sophisticated, motor cars scarce, and social events almost impossible to attend. If they wanted an evening out, there were few people brave enough to take on the responsibilities of the energetic twins. Both Nellie and William had always been avid readers, so they began reading the classics aloud to each other. This diversion soon became part of their daily life. As the boys grew older, they would stop and listen to their parents' voices, and eventually began reading with them. The whole family found joy in books and shared companionship.

With their family growing and money problems behind them, Nellie and William began to entertain his clients and attend social events. Nellie joined an exclusive woman's club so she would have a life outside of her home. She had always been afraid of public speaking, and at first it was difficult for her to actively participate at the meetings. Within the friendly circle of women, Nellie eventually learned to put fear aside and became an eloquent speaker. This accomplishment was to be beneficial in the years ahead.

Although Nellie had never been an aggressive woman, she was extremely interested in her husband's law practice as well as the politics of the party. Nellie became his critic and admirer; she knew his problems and desires. Every aspect of William's career was valuable to her and through him Nellie learned how to deal with the problems of the law. William began calling her his "safe repository." He could confide his affairs freely and knew they would go no further.

In 1912, the Rosses were delighted with the birth of a new son, Bradford. Their financial problems were over and Nellie had all the household help she needed. They had time to enjoy their new baby and continue an active social life. Part of William's ambitions had been fulfilled. He had a happy family life, successful law practice, and was recognized as a leading member of the Democratic Party. Nellie was also content. She was satisfied being a wife, mother, and homemaker.

In 1922, their lives completely changed when William was nominated for governor of the state of Wyoming. At first Nellie strenuously resisted his candidacy. Although the power and dignity of the office were alluring, she did not want William to abandon his lucrative law practice that had taken years to build. Nellie enjoyed her lifestyle and the twins were in college with needs that multiplied daily. But all the while she protested, Nellie knew in her heart she had no right to hold her husband back from all he had worked so hard to achieve. She finally decided to gracefully back his nomination and William ran for the office of governor. The family would have to learn to budget and live on the low pay of a politician.

Once she committed, Nellie gave her husband her full support, and she did so with pride. Within a day, William hit the campaign trail while his wife remained home to rally support from their friends and associates. William ran on the progressive ticket and his own integrity. At the end of three months, when the last vote was counted, William Bradford Ross won the election — the glamorous life of a politician's wife was about to begin.

The next few weeks were filled with activity. As they packed for the move to the Governor's Mansion, the Rosses remembered the many happy years spent in their own modest home. Nellie had mixed emotions. She was glad her husband had fulfilled his dreams, but afraid that the responsibilities ahead were more than she could handle. There was little time to dwell upon her fears, however, for she had many changes to oversee in the mansion that would better serve the needs of her family. William also expected her help with his inaugural address. He rarely gave a speech without Nellie's approval.

As final plans for the Inaugural Ceremony approached, Nellie was at a loss as to what to wear to the Ball. When it came to clothing, she always let her husband make the final decision. Nellie considered his taste to be impeccable — and she was right. With his help, the Governor's Lady was the most beautifully dressed woman of the evening.

The family found their new residence to be both elegant and

comfortable, and Nellie's former doubts were put to rest. She knew they would be delighted with their new lifestyle.What she had once considered to be beyond her ability turned out to be a glamorous and interesting period in her life. There were state functions, dinners, and receptions for officials. Nellie was a gracious hostess who warmly welcomed everyone to her home.

Within a few weeks Nellie became close to the office of her husband. The problems of his administration and the people who worked for him became familiar to her. The same interest she had shown during their marriage was as strong as ever. Nellie was always there to assist when necessary. William not only loved his wife, he appreciated her intelligence as well, and often praised her to his associates. He was an honorable man and his reputation as a good governor was growing throughout the state.

Then, after 20 years of a wonderful life, fate stepped in and dealt the family a devastating blow. William became seriously ill and underwent an appendectomy on September 25. On October 2, 1924, at the age of 51, he passed away. Overnight, the stately mansion that was filled with happiness became a place of mourning—William Bradford Ross, the 12th governor of Wyoming was gone. His passing left a void that was felt throughout the state.

The sudden loss of her husband filled Nellie with despair and a sorrow deeper than she had ever known. Her love and companionship with William had been the supreme interest and joy of her married life. His death left her lost. She missed the good, strong man who would no longer be by her side. During all their years together Nellie's individuality had merged with his — now she was incomplete, alone with an unknown future.

Almost immediately, Mrs. Ross was asked to allow her name to be presented to the voters of Wyoming as a candidate to fill her husband's unfinished term, and Nellie was both dismayed and bewildered. She spoke at great length with her brother but when her converstation ended she was still confused. However, as members of the party began talking about what William's death would mean to the State of Wyoming, Nellie realized it was a time of emergency. With the counsel of her family and the feeling that her husband would want her to carry on his work, she finally accepted the nomination.

Nellie Tayloe Ross's name was formally filed with the secretary of state as the Democratic candidate for governor of the State of Wyoming. Although she rarely left the privacy of her home during the campaign, her life began to take on a new meaning. Nellie later said: "It was like a birth into a new world that moved me from loneliness and solitude to a battle for the highest office in the state" — something no other women had dared to do.

The first repercussions came from the appalling publicity. Most newspapers thought she was insane — no doubt a reflection of the male attitude of the day. As news of the nomination spread around the country, all forms of stories were circulated; a woman candidate elicited more than a little attention. Nellie's personal affairs were paraded before the public and her opinion on all subjects was in demand, and then misquoted. Reporters asked everything from the size of her shoes to the size of her dresses. They dug out old photos of Nellie dressed in what she considered long-forgotten styles, and she was embarrassed. Finally one news man went too far when he requested a photo of her making bread while wearing an apron. Nellie gave him a definite no, and he left in defeat. She had had enough.

Mrs. Ross ran on her husband's platform. She pledged to do everything in her power to carry on his programs and declared to the women voters that, if elected, she would devote herself to excellent service on their behalf. The women believed her and the people of Wyoming had approved of her late husband's policies. While in office he had gained their respect; the voters knew Nellie had worked beside him, and they felt she would keep her promises.

On the day of the election Nellie voted early with her two older sons by her side. Since they had reached their majority, each cast his first vote for his mother. Then the family returned to the executive mansion. There, from behind the curtains of the large, quiet house, Nellie watched the people enter the polls, and she wondered how it would all turn out. She eventually retired to her bedroom and in solitude waited for the results. As the first phone calls began, Nellie tried not to become overconfident. When the call she had been waiting for finally arrived — it was a landslide victory for the lady candidate — Nellie Tayloe Ross had been elected to serve as the first woman governor of Wyoming and thus became the first woman governor in the nation.

On the day of the inauguration, January 5, 1925, the senate chamber was so filled that people were standing in the halls and up and down the stairs. There was a cameraman in place to record the important event in a moving picture. On January 6, 1925, the *Wyoming State Tribune* gave this report: "A few minutes after 12:00 noon the doors to the rear of the rostrum opened and Chief Justice Potter entered followed by Mrs. Ross on the arm of her brother, Judge Samuel Tayloe, of San Antonio, Texas" . . . her two sons, George and Bradford, were behind their mother. . . . "Mrs. Ross, gowned in black with widow's hat and black veil that fell to her waistline, and wearing gloves, then delivered her partly memorized, partly read address. . . . Justice Potter delivered the oath of office as she placed her hand on the Bible." And the brief ceremony was over. The new lady governor was on her own to face the scrutiny of Wyoming and the eyes of the nation — everything she did would be recorded.

There were many people that day who wondered what Mrs. Ross was thinking as she took her oath. Nellie later wrote that her mind went back to that day two years before when her husband stood in the same place to take the same oath. Only then, she had been by his side — was he, she wondered, now standing unseen and silent beside her?

The following day, the editor of the *Laramie Republic and Boomerang* wrote two columns about the impressive ceremony. One described Mrs. Ross as having a "Lincolnian quality" and the other stated that she appeared to be a "leader of uncommon ability." Several newspapers called her "The Lady in Black," and others refused to comment, waiting to see what the new governor would do.

Nellie knew she was neither a crusader nor a martyr. She had always been a straight-forward intelligent woman and she had no doubts about her ability to govern the state. Only loneliness prevailed as she took up the affairs of her new office and calmly prepared to follow her husband's path, a woman Democrat in the heart of a masculine Republican stronghold.

In May 1925, a *Good Housekeeping* article read: "On March 3, 1925, America had its first glimpse of the nation's first woman governor when she attended the inauguration of President Coolidge. Later, Governor Ross rode in the parade carrying a small Wyoming flag and received, perhaps, the greatest ovation of all — a woman governor in an inaugural parade."

Following her appearance in the parade, cartoons sprang up all over the country. One artist drew a picture of Nellie riding into the city on a bucking bronco, wearing a cowgirl costume. Another presented her as a stern mother, shaking her fist at a small-boy legislature and telling them what to do. The caption read, "frills, frailties, foibles and follies." The fact that she was a woman was a challenge, but Governor Ross saw the humor and smiled to herself as she went on with her duties.

During her term in office Governor Ross never played politics as it was usually played. She was a governor, not a politician, and she was successful. Although many men dodged the important issues, the lady went out to meet them and settled the problems.

When a sheriff was accused of being hand-in-glove with bootleggers, Ross went to battle. She had never been in a courtroom in her life, but she held the hearing as prescribed by law and made her ruling without flinching. The sheriff was relieved of his duties and there was more rapport for Nellie that day than ever before. Governor Ross proved she was a woman who knew how to govern — the gentle lady was applauded by all, except perhaps the unemployed sheriff.

Many other bills were brought before the Governor and she carefully battled her way through each separate one, always trying to follow the will of her constituents. When the economy caused 120 banks to fail, she fought to have a bank examiner appointed so the people of her state would feel secure putting their hard-earned money in savings accounts. While Nellie was in office she also cut the expense of government considerably: "Like the good and careful homemaker that she was before she was chosen governor, she had, in public office, observed the same wise economies."

During the two years of her term, Ross conducted her office in a dignified and highly creditable manner. She met the demands with courage, yet lost none of her feminine charm. Mrs. Ross was not involved in what would later be called women's lib; she felt if she performed her duties in a capable manner, setting an example for success, other women would be more likely to follow her path. Unfortunately, the suffragettes did not appreciate what she did; they felt she should have replaced her husband's male appointments with women, something she would not even consider. Nellie did put women in positions of trust during her administration, but only if the opportunity arose.

When it was time to run for re-election, Governor Ross once again accepted the nomination. She campaigned strenuously for several weeks, canvassing the state in a Hudson automobile, speaking in as many as seven towns in one day. As record crowds turned out to hear her speak, she pointed out the beauty of Wyoming as well as the achievements of her administration. When she returned to the capital

Nellie was exhausted. It had been hard work, and now time would tell if it was enough.

Although Nellie had many successes that directly influenced women, it was the suffragettes who voted against her second term. She was doubly damned. The antifeminists disparaged her for being a woman and the libbers condemned her for not appointing more women. Her defeat was inevitable for she could not serve both groups. The surprise was that she lost by a very small margin.

After her defeat, Nellie Ross never again ran for office, but she did not lose interest in politics. Nellie became active in the Democratic National Committee and a popular speaker. From 1927 to 1932, she worked diligently for her party. In 1933, President Franklin D. Roosevelt, who had been following her career with interest, broke precedent and appointed Mrs. Nellie Ross as director of the United States Mint. Once again this amazing woman had captured another "first woman" distinction.

As director of the Mint, she had eight houses to keep: the Bureau of the Mint in Washington; coin factories in Denver, San Francisco, and Philadelphia; assay offices in New York and Seattle; and two depositories — one for gold at Fort Knox and one for silver at West Point. It could be said she was the keeper of a gold and silver empire.

The job was complex and difficult. When Nellie took over in 1933, activity was low at the Mint due to the Depression. During World War II it grew to over 4,000 specialized employees working 24-hours a day. Nellie not only proved to be a capable director, but also made important improvements. She was an accomplished lady with a sharp mind.

While under her administration, Mrs. Ross's efficiency saved taxpayers money and they, in turn, were happy with her performance. She blazed a trail of public service — with a perfect record. Due to the excellence of her management, other states began to select women for posts of great responsibilities. In her own way, Nellie, as director of the Mint, was a quiet champion of women's rights and made it a point to help each individual. She hired many women, some for high positions, and her female employees, as well as the male, had the opportunity to work from secretaries to top administrators.

During her years as "Mrs. Money," the senators enjoyed calling Nellie without warning to ask how many tons of gold were at Fort Knox, as well as how she knew it was there, and when she last saw it.

Her firm reply was usually the same, "If I were as certain of everything as I am our gold and silver, wouldn't I find it a perfect world to live in." She was always ready to answer a question and ran the Mint as she ran a home — on a budget. One newspaper declared "Hurray for Nellie! As a taxpayer, I love her." She was affectionately called "Our Nell."

Nellie spent over 20 years in Washington, D.C. She lived in a large, comfortable apartment filled with elegant furnishings and ornate Oriental rugs. She liked to surround herself with beautiful things and mementos of her past. As a woman holding one of the few high positions in Washington, Mrs. Ross was popular in the social life of the capital and admitted she loved the people and the many parties.

In 1953, at the age of 77, Nellie Ross finally retired from the Mint. She had served four five-year terms, a real record for a woman who never had any desire for public office.

During all her years in Washington, Nellie always considered herself to be a Westerner. She visited Wyoming frequently and maintained a residence in Cheyenne. After retirement Nellie continued to contribute to women's magazines and kept active in politics. She traveled around the country on speaking engagements, and when in Washington, she found herself surrounded by old friends, her sons, and grandchildren. Nellie was never lonely, nor idle.

On December 19, 1977, Nellie Tayloe Ross quietly passed away in her home in Washington, D.C., at the age of 101. Her funeral services were held at St. Mark's Episcopal Church of Cheyenne, Wyoming. Nellie was buried in the West she had loved and served so well. She will always be remembered as a pioneer for women's rights and for her outstanding accomplishments. Mrs. Ross was truly one of the great women in American history.

THE WYOMING EAGLE
Cheyenne, December 21, 1977
EDITORIAL COMMENT
One of the Great Women in American History

"It was coincidental but fitting that the birthday of women's suffrage and the birthday of Nellie Tayloe Ross should have come so close to falling on the same date. One hundred and eight years ago, Dec. 10, 1869, Wyoming territorial Gov. Campbell signed into law the Woman Suffrage Act which was to earn for Wyoming the nickname, "Equality State." Just a little less than seven years later, Nov. 29, 1876, Nellie Tayloe Ross, who was to earn the nickname, "Mrs. Equality," was born. A few days ago, this state observed Wyoming Day, 1977 — the 108th anniversary of women's suffrage. Today, Wyoming mourns the death of Nellie Tayloe Ross of Wyoming, first woman governor in America, first woman director of the U.S. Mint, former vice chairman of the Democratic National Committee, lecturer and campaigner. Mrs. Ross died Monday in Washington, D.C., at the age of 101. Funeral services will be at 2 p.m. today at St. Mark's Episcopal Church of Cheyenne. The Rev. Eugene Todd will officiate and burial will be in Lakeview."

Courtesy of The Wyoming State Archives, Department of State Parks and Resources

William Bradford Ross

Nellie's husband

Courtesy of The Wyoming State Archives, Department of State Parks and Resources

Nellie Tayloe Ross

The Honorable Nellie Tayloe Ross
Signing the oath of office

Inaugural Statement
of Nellie Tayloe Ross

My Friends:

Owing to the tragic and unprecedented circumstances which surround my induction into office, I have felt it not only unnecessary but inappropriate for me now to enter into such a discussion of policies as usually constitutes an inaugural address.

This occasion does not mark the beginning of a new administration, but rather the resumption of that which was inaugurated in this chamber two years ago. It is well understood, I am sure, that it is my purpose to continue, as I am convinced it is the desire of my state that I should, insofar as changing conditions will permit, the program and policies then launched.

I avail myself of this opportunity to acknowledge the gracious consideration shown me by Governor Lucas during the period he has served as Chief Executive of our State, and to say that I look forward confidently to that same degree of cooperation with him and with the other state officers and with the legislature that during my husband's term lightened for him the burdens of official life and contributed to his satisfaction and joy in service.

In approaching the responsibilities of this exalted office, I do so with a profound sense of the high obligation it imposes upon me. That the people of Wyoming should have placed such trust in me — in large measure, I feel, an expression of their recognition of my husband's devotion to their interests, and of his contribution to the progress of the state — calls forth in this solemn hour my deepest gratitude, and challenges me to rise to the opportunities for service thus made possible, and to dedicate to the task before me every faculty of mind and body with which I may be endowed.

Such dedication I now offer to my state, relying upon Divine help for strength and guidance.

CAPITOL BUILDiNG—CHEYENNE.

NELLIE TAYLOE ROSS—EX-GOVERNOR OF WYOMING AND THE FIRST WOMAN GOVERNOR OF THE UNITED STATES.

Courtesy of The Wyoming State Archives, Department of State Parks and Resources

Nellie Tayloe Ross
Governor of Wyoming, 1925 - 1927

The story of Nellie Taylor Ross's ascension to a place in history is not one of an ambitious suffragette. Although she was a trail-blazer for women in politics, she always spoke of the woman's role at home as a more noble one. As she grew older, the energetic woman never lost her interest in life and politics. She cherished her memorable past yet lived in the present — always a fascinating lovely lady who was active until the end. . . .

Speaker Underwood's Tribute
To the First Woman Governor

At the adjournment of the last session of the State Legislature, in response to the address of Governor Nellie Tayloe Ross, bidding farewell to the Legislature, Hon. J. C. Underwood, Republican, Speaker of the House, who has served in that body for many years, under many governors, recognized the ability of the first woman governor with these words: "Governor Ross, those of us who have had the privilege to participate for several sessions in the work of the Legislature know how exacting and onerous are the duties which a session thrusts upon the Governor. I want to say to you that in my experience no Governor has handled these duties with greater courtesy, with greater accuracy or with more ability."

Colorado G. O. P. Chairman
Says Governor Has Made Good

Speaking at the meeting of the Republican State Committee in Casper only a few months ago, the leader of the Republican party in Colorado, State Chairman John Coen, thus acknowledged the ability of the first woman governor: "Your state at this time fills a unique position in that the office of chief magistrate is filled by one who represents all that is best in the womanhood of Wyoming. While she claims allegiance to a political faith to which we cannot subscribe, no woman has done more to dignify a place in public life or to justify full suffrage for women and equal participation in public affairs." The Republican leader was right. Nellie Tayloe Ross is the woman who made good. She deserves re-election.
— Wyoming Labor Journal, Cheyenne.

May Arkwright Hutton

She hitched her wagon to a star.

Chapter 6

MAY ARKWRIGHT HUTTON
AN UNCONVENTIONAL WOMAN

Despite her boisterous behavior, outrageous attire, and ability to upset the "proper" ladies, May Hutton became one of the most noted women of the Pacific Northwest. May's generosity to the less fortunate changed many lives — her contributions to suffrage helped the women of both Idaho and Washington receive the right to vote.

May Arkwright was born in July 1860, in the coal mining district of Washingtonville, Ohio. Her father Isaac Arkwright, according to most records, was a professional wanderer who never stayed in one place long enough to raise a family. May's mother deserted him when May was a small child. Her father soon tired of dragging his daughter around with him, and left the ten-year-old child to be raised by his blind father.

For many years the bewildered Grandpa Arkwright became the only family May knew. His attitude toward the young charge was one of acceptance without love. She cooked, cleaned, and led her grandfather around town. He was an opinionated man who was actively involved in politics as well as many issues of the day. It was from Grandpa Arkwright that May developed her intense interest in what she felt were matters of great importance.

The old man and the young girl settled into what for them was a normal lifestyle. May managed to attend school off and on and acquired a brief education. There wasn't a lot of money or affection in the Arkwright home, but May learned to survive and do without. Her clothes were plain and her life was simple. She had always been a large girl, and as May grew to maturity and filled out, she realized she would always be a heavy person who enjoyed cooking and eating. May also knew she would always be able to take care of herself.

Details of her early years are vague. During the time she lived with her grandfather, May learned from the family Bible that her father had four other children. She had three half-brothers and one half-sister. After a brief search, May found their addresses and began to communicate with them. These new relationships appeared to play a very important role in her life for it meant she was part of a real family.

The young woman and her grandfather drifted along in their unusual way of life for several years. May continued to cook and clean for him as well as others, and she eventually opened a boarding house. During that time May developed a boisterous, outgoing personality and an avid interest in politics.

In her early 20s, May decided to leave Grandpa Arkwright and the grimness of Ohio's coal mines behind. She packed a few clothes in what has been described as a large wicker basket, and joined a group of prospectors heading for the rich mines of the Coeur d'Alenes in Idaho. May Arkwright was moving West, where the newspapers claimed there was gold for those ambitious enough to pick it up off the ground.

When this strange group of 40 men and one large woman arrived in Rathdrum, Idaho, they must have made quite an impression upon its citizens. What the people thought, however, didn't matter to May. She was strong, healthy, and filled with a burning desire for a better life.

The ambitious young woman managed to land her first job as a cook in the mining community of Eagle, one of the earliest towns in the placer area. Eagle was comprised of tents and shacks set on lots that had been carefully laid out. Food prices were high, liquor plentiful, and the ladies of negotiable virtue were eager to take the miners' money. It was there May tied an apron around her ample waist and began to cook. Her reputation for excellent food and sharp wit soon spread beyond the mining camp.

When the mines around Eagle began to fail, May was hired by Jim Wardner to cook at Wardner's Junction. The miners followed and business flourished. May was a respected no-nonsense woman who learned to listen and use her own mind. Her hands were work-worn, her body sturdy, and her laughter coarse, but the men were fond of her. May's love of cooking and her well-padded body were a comforting sight that made the miners think of their own homes and families, so many miles away. They came to eat and stayed to visit.

May finally tired of working for someone else, and decided to open her own restaurant in a two-room shack. With a mop, and a bucket, and a lot of cleaning she was ready to open her door. The front section of the shack served as a dining area and was furnished with an oilcloth-covered table, and a stove set in the corner. The back room became the bedroom. May kept a rain barrel and strong soap handy to insure cleanliness, and a scrub board for washing clothes. Her restaurant had a homey atmosphere and the aroma of fine food filled the air. It was a place where the men were well fed and able to share a joke with their hostess.

May continued to cook and the men continued to flock in the door. She bought a cow for fresh milk, and began washing the men's laundry and mending their clothing. The days were long and the nights too short, but May was making money without working in the mines. Her plain face and friendly personality made everyone feel welcome, even the soiled doves who worked down the street. Perhaps it was the fancy clothing those "ladies" wore that influenced May in her taste for bright colors, ruffles, bows, and feathers. The little girl, who never had love or pretty things, developed a taste for flamboyant attire that lacked style and often set her apart from the other women.

One busy day, May noticed the quiet engineer who had been stopping daily to eat. Although he was known as Al, his name was Levi W. Hutton, and it was obvious he enjoyed May's cooking. As the months went by, they became close friends. He was fascinated by her lusty love of life and joy of cooking. May admired his neat appearance and decency; he was a man she knew she could respect.

Although their personalities were totally different, they shared a similar background. Al had been orphaned at six, and raised on an Iowa farm by an unloving uncle who overworked the boy and denied him an education. He left the farm as soon as he was old enough and by the time he was 22, Al had moved up from laborer to locomotive engineer for the Northern Pacific Railroad. Al and May were self-made people and both were 27 when he proposed. May might have been considered large and overbearing by some, but Al knew he loved her with all of his heart.

They were married in 1887, with a large group of friends attending the ceremony. People came from all over the Coeur d'Alenes by foot, horseback, wagon, and locomotive. The happy bride wore a fussy blue dress with ruffles, and an apron tied around her waist. She had prepared the wedding feast and the tables were overflowing. As they took their vows, Al, in a plain suit, stood quietly beside his bride. He was happier than anyone could remember seeing him.

Once she was married, the new Mrs. Hutton took her role as a respected housewife seriously. They moved into a two-room house in Wallace, which was their first step up the ladder of success. May, however, was not accepted by the "elite" of Wallace. She had been a cook, washerwoman, and above all, she was uneducated. Her outrageous taste in clothing, ribald sense of humor, and assertive personality didn't fit in.

Although Mrs. Hutton tried as hard as she could to break into their circle, she failed. Within a short time May realized they would never be her friends. If the ladies didn't want her, she decided she would just find something else to do. From then on, it appears May Hutton became her own person — she no longer sought the approval of others.

May opened a dining room in the Wallace Hotel and did a booming business. She became active in union affairs, women's suffrage and began reading. Soon she was writing letters and poetry, something she enjoyed. In one of her letters to her brother, May confided that at one time she felt more comfortable with the 40 miners with whom she came West than she ever did with just one man, but Al was different. The minute she met him, his gentleness won her heart.

The Huttons enjoyed many social activities. Al belonged to the Masonic Lodge, and it was an important part of his life. He was also a member of the Elks and Oddfellows and the couple, especially May, enjoyed attending the many dances. They provided an opportunity for her to dress to the nines in one of her flamboyant gowns. Needless to say, her low cut dresses, which showed an ample bosom, often shocked the ladies — of course none of that bothered May anymore, and she happily danced the night away.

For many years both Al and May had invested in what they called "holes" in the canyons, always hoping to strike it rich. When the chance arose to buy a share in a claim called the Hercules, they talked it over and put up $880 with a promise that Al would work off the rest, digging in the mine with the other partners. May often joined the men as they worked, and on those occasions she always wore a pair of male overalls. Both the Huttons knew it was a long shot to put so much money in a mine, but then so was life.

Shortly after her marriage, May met Abigail Scott Duniway,

who was in Idaho to help the women gain the right to vote. Abigail was a well-known suffragist, and May saw in her the same dedication for women's rights that she felt. The women became friends and started working together to promote their cause. In 1896, when the men of Idaho gave women the vote, May pledged to help Mrs. Duniway continue suffrage in Oregon.

Problems at the mines, however, began to worsen, so May wasn't able to join her friend in Oregon. The miners were dissatisfied with their working conditions and low pay. Mrs. Hutton became an outspoken advocate for the Western Federation of Miners, which was attempting to organize the Coeur d'Alenes. The men's frustration finally came to a head. On April 29, 1899, at Burke, Idaho, a group of approximately 150 miners seized the train on which Al Hutton was the engineer. Two masked men, armed with revolvers, ordered him to take the train to Wardner, where the Bunker Hill and Sullivan concentrator was located. Al had no recourse but to comply.

The angry men planned to dynamite the mill, and they did. Although Al had no choice in the affair, he was incarcerated with the guilty men in a stockade that was called "the bull pen." They were all put under guard by federal troops, and May was furious. She had hated the mine owners for years because of their greed and lack of interest in the needs of their workers. This gave her a chance to spew out all of her pent-up anger — they had gone too far when her Al was treated like a common criminal.

First, May pleaded for her husband's freedom, and then she created several disturbances with the guards. Her abusive words were so annoying they hated to see her come near the stockade, and often made uncomplimentary remarks behind her back. Although Al was released before the other men, Mrs. Hutton was still furious. She wrote lengthy letters to the governor of Idaho, the *Spokesman Review,* and any other newspaper that would print them. Then she decided to write a book, *The Coeur d'Alenes, a Tale of Modern Inquisition in Idaho.*

May's book was an unbelievable narrative of angry words that showed the amount of hatred she felt over Al's arrest. She invented outlandish names for all who were involved in the affair, which fooled no one, and she extolled the virtues of the unions. The book sold over 8,000 copies and May gained a reputation she found hard to live down. To make matters worse, the book was dedicated, "To my husband, who is an innocent man, arrested and confined to the bull pen for days in an effort to coerce him into giving testimony. . . ." Even Al felt that was a bit hard to live with!

In 1901, the unbelievable happened when the Hercules Mine in which the Huttons invested began showing a small profit. The investors, described in the newspapers as the grocer, schoolteacher, barber, milkman, and engineer, had beaten the odds. These diligent men and women, who had borrowed when the money ran out and carefully worked each lead, no matter how disappointing, had won! The final assays revealed a rich vein and the happy partners celebrated at the Huttons', where May cooked an enormous dinner. Later, they decided to work the mine themselves.

Then, in 1902, the Hercules Mine again surprised everyone when it turned out to be worth millions. The uneducated, hardworking couple found themselves wealthy beyond their wildest dreams. The Hercules had become what was called a real "Glory Hole," and the *Wallace Free Press* believed it to be the richest silver ore ever found.

With more money than they knew what to do with, the Huttons moved into a larger house, where May could entertain properly. Since she had never lost her love of cooking and food, the dining room became the focal point of their home. May would spread a lace tablecloth over a massive table, lay out her fine silver and crystal, and head for the kitchen. The Huttons' guests were always welcomed by their hostess who prepared and served the meal herself; no one ever left hungry.

Although the society ladies of Wallace still chose to ignore Mrs. Hutton, Al was welcomed everywhere. May must have been hurt, but she never showed it. She claimed there were more important things to do than worry about what others thought.

There was a constant flow of out-of-town visitors at the Huttons'. It was not unusual to see well-known attorneys, union leaders, and leading suffragettes enjoying May's hospitality. Even Teddy Roosevelt stopped for dinner while he was touring the West. If the elite society of Wallace wanted to remain aloof, they were welcome to do so. There were many who sought the company of the Huttons. There was one problem May had to live with, however: her book. It was a direct insult to the mine owners, and she had become one. It was said that Mrs. Hutton traveled all over buying back as many books as possible. Today they are considered a collector's item.

May began to send money to her Arkwright relatives in Ohio; she loved them and wanted to share her wealth. An attorney successfully located her mother and May enclosed a check in every letter she wrote to her. Both of the Huttons were generous. Al gave to the Masonic Lodge and churches, and May gave to the women's rights groups and schools. Anyone in need knew they would get a handout from those kind people who would never forget the less fortunate.

Eventually, the Huttons decided to leave the Coeur d'Alenes and move to the community of Spokane, Washington. May needed a place to enlarge her political power. Like a gaudy rooster who had outgrown his old henhouse, May was looking for a new nest. Al was also ready to move up. He had become an investor who wanted to spread his wings.

Mrs. Hutton hit Spokane with a splash. She was like an unpolished gem with great potential. From the start, May refused to take on the role of an ordinary woman — her buoyant personality couldn't be confined within the walls of one house. She had to be part of all she deemed to be important. When her wild, extravagant clothing became too outrageous or her assertive personality aroused too much criticism, Al would quietly say, "Don't make a show of yourself, May," and surprisingly, she took his advice.

Spokane, like May, was determined to grow. Most of the money from the rich mines of the Coeur d'Alenes was finding its way to this city. The newly rich silver barons built their elegant homes on the tree-studded mountainsides, and the merchants were becoming wealthy. The society women were trying to create an image of gentility in their city, and May Hutton was a disruption they hadn't planned on.

Unlike the conventional members of this new elite society, who lived in normal houses, the Huttons' first home was a nine-room penthouse on the top floor of Al's new downtown building. This raised more than one eyebrow. May traveled all over the nation buying the most expensive furniture she could find. Unfortunately, she never lost her gaudy taste. Her home was a colorful assortment of elegant things that didn't match.

Al bought a scarlet Thomas Flyer, and with a chauffeur at her command, May could be seen all over town with the ostrich feathers from her hat flying in the wind. In the growing city that was attempting to prove its sophistication, Mrs. Hutton was considered an embarrassment. The fact that it was her generosity to the derelicts and prostitutes that kept them off the streets went unnoticed.

Mrs. Hutton became a celebrity; reporters seemed to respect

the large, often uncouth, woman who made good copy. She said what she thought and was always ready to write a check for a worthy cause. May moved in her own independent world. There were many issues that needed to be dealt with and she was ready to take them on.

One of her commitments was to help the Florence Crittenden Home for unwed mothers. To May, an unwed mother was not a sinner, for after all she wasn't sure of her own mother's marital status before she was born. May embraced these unfortunate women and their babies in her big, wide-open arms. She knew they had only made a mistake; they were not "bad." Her world was one of goodness and her love was so great it included all people.

At first, May merely wrote checks to help the Home, but eventually she became a member of the board of directors. It wasn't long before Mrs. Hutton had the entire board in an uproar. May wanted to know why the Crittenden Home was a shelter for mothers before their babies were placed in an orphanage, and not a place where the woman could learn to make a home for herself and her child. She considered the family, not just the mother. May wanted each woman to learn to care for her baby, train for a job, and hopefully become a housewife. For the latter, May already had plans that would further upset the board.

The surrounding countryside was filled with lonely ranchers who needed good wives. Since her "girls" and their babies needed homes, May decided Crittendens should set up a matrimonial agency. This outrageous idea shocked the directors so much that their protests were heard throughout Spokane. Who did this outspoken woman think she was? It was said the idea was out of the question; it was preposterous. May, however, went on with her business of creating new lives for the mothers and infants.

In theory, May's plan could have been a success. She set up carefully chaperoned meetings between the couples in order for them to get acquainted. If one of the couples decided to get married, May paid for the wedding and Al assisted by giving the bride away. A few weddings did occur, and for those newlyweds it was not unusual for May to help them set up housekeeping. If May's scheme had been successful, Spokane would have had fewer orphans, leaving the society ladies looking for a new "cause."

May had a special interest in suffrage; it was her pet project. She was a woman of great wealth and power, but in Washington, she could not control her own destiny. In 1896, May had been instrumental in achieving the vote for the women of Idaho, now she felt it was time to work with the suffragettes of Washington. However, May Hutton seldom worked "with" anyone for long. With her strident personality and large checkbook, she usually took over leadership.

Within a short time, May replaced Mrs. DeVoe, the president of the State Association of Suffragettes, and the group moved ahead. This move created a lot of animosity between the two women. Mrs. DeVoe claimed Mrs. Hutton was unfit to lead the Association, but May chose to ignore her accusations for the good of all involved. The ladies knew the initiative had to be placed on the ballot for the 1910 general election, and there was no time to spare.

May offered to pay the cost of sending eight, highly motivated women to the state capital in Olympia, with herself as their leader. When her offer was accepted, May rented the lower floor of the Hoar Mansion in that city for their headquarters and the women, dressed in their finest, went to work. Before the convention was over, their bill was placed on the ballot. With victory in Olympia, the ladies had several months to convince the men to vote for suffrage.

Antifeminist cartoons began to appear in the newspapers, but the women ignored them and forged ahead. These dedicated ladies were ready to fight for the right to vote, and with Mrs. Hutton in their lead, Heaven help any man who stood in their way. May sponsored dinners for leading politicians who she felt would help their cause. She even hired a newspaperwoman from Denver to publicize suffrage in Washington. Each article, no matter how large or small, was sent over the wire service.

May's scarlet Flyer, covered with colorful posters, could be seen canvassing the state from one end to the other, often with Mrs. Duniway, Carrie Chapman Catt, or other popular suffragettes sitting by her side. It was a whirlwind campaign with dedicated women working together. On November 8, 1910, the ladies won when the male voters passed suffrage by a margin of almost two to one. After the election, Mrs. Hutton was honored at a reception in Spokane, where she thanked all the women for their hard work.

May had gained a name for herself in the political arena, and in 1912, she became the first woman delegate from Spokane to attend the Democratic Convention in Baltimore, Maryland. This was an honor that Mrs. Hutton had never dreamed possible. It was said that once May was seated at the convention, she never left her place, despite the unusually hot, humid weather.

When the day was over, May returned to her hotel where, according to the media, she washed her large undies and hung them out of the window to dry. They must have created quite an uproar, flapping in the breeze. When the irate manager requested the lady delegate from Washington to remove her unmentionables from the window, May replied she had rented the room and the window went with it — needless to say, the undergarments continued to fly.

In sophisticated Baltimore, Mrs. Hutton was not shunned by society as she had been in Wallace and Spokane. Despite her flamboyant attire and outspoken personality, she was welcomed everywhere. May was a sought-after speaker and honored guest at the country club. *The Boston Sun* declared that suffrage in Washington was passed "largely through Mrs. Hutton's efforts." As stories of May's success in Baltimore spread West, the people who had once laughed at her must have felt more than a little uncomfortable and perhaps a bit of envy.

When May returned to Spokane she wasn't feeling well, but refused to see a doctor; there were too many things to do. She was on a roll and it was a good time for a party. Although Mrs. Hutton had proven her political ability and done so many things to help others, she still received catty remarks from certain women. On the evening of her party, May's special guest of honor was one of her favorite actresses; it was a special night. As Mrs. Hutton stood beside her guest in the receiving line, an old acquaintance from her Wallace days smiled and commented, "I believe my husband boarded with you in the Coeur d'Alenes." Without batting an eye, May replied, "Yes he did, and what's more, he is one of the few boarders that walked out on his bill." May had the ability to either ignore an uncomplimentary remark, or turn it into one that made the other person look like a fool. If her feelings were hurt, she never let anyone know.

Mrs. Hutton loved the many plays, operas, and vaudeville shows that appeared in Spokane. Her ample form, decked out in colorful splendor, was often seen on opening nights. Al always managed to reserve a box near the stage for his wife and her friends. It was said that one night May became so sentimental that her sobbing during a performance disturbed an actor so much he forgot his lines. Since May enjoyed the theatre, she would always help a performer in need. She was known to have paid the train fare home for several young entertainers who were stranded in Spokane.

Although Al was the quiet partner in their marriage, he was also

May's strength. Mr. Hutton was a respected businessman in the community and, like his wife, he was always ready to help build a new church or lend a helping hand, only he did it silently. May often said when her Al put his foot down, she knew he was the boss. She claimed it would be impossible to be married to a man who couldn't make her mind. Her devotion to Al was obvious. The two of them complemented, protected, and appreciated each other.

May's friends were also important to her. When she wrote to them they were always addressed, "My Dear Wee Lady," "My Dear Dear Honey Bun," or "Dear Girlie." She was sincerely fond of these ladies and her letters were frank and affectionate. Their feelings toward her were never discussed. If they laughed behind her back, she never found out.

May continued to lose her strength and often complained that she was "just bone tired." Al began to notice his robust wife's failing health and expressed his concern. When May finally went to see a doctor, he told her to change her eating habits and take things easy. She told him, "I'll eat what I darn well please and do what I want," and stalked out. Although May's health continued to decline, she said she was fine and just needed a little rest.

In 1914, Al decided to build his May a new home, thinking it might perk her up, and it did for a brief period. She immediately started to design a mansion with white pillars, a huge veranda, and the most fashionable furnishings she could buy. Al had always wanted a cow, and their property was large enough to accommodate one. Despite the thrill of a new home, May continued to lose her weight as well as her strength. After visiting a series of doctors she was diagnosed with Bright's Disease and told she had to diet and take care of herself. And she did, in the only way she knew how; May had a housewarming for over 1,000 guests. This time she became so ill there were nurses and doctors all over the place.

May improved a little, and Al took her to a natural healer in California. When that didn't help they sought spiritual guidance, but May continued to fail. Mrs. Hutton began to lose her appetite and remained in her room most of the time. When her favorite politician, William Jennings Bryan, the future U.S. senator, found out his friend was ill, he left his travels to pay the lady a visit. This helped May so much she decided to have a lawn party for the 1,000 politicians attending the Washington State Federation of Women's Clubs Convention.

When Mrs. Hutton greeted her guests, dressed in a fancy new gown, she was sitting in a wheelchair. Although her laughter was as loud as ever and her jokes were as amusing, it was obvious to everyone that their hostess was not well. She resembled an old warrior who wanted to conquer new territory, but was just too tired to make the effort. It was the last time the memorable May Hutton would ever give a party.

While May continued her fight for survival, Al was constantly by her side. He gave up his business meetings, the Lodge, and the card games he so enjoyed. Al even bought May a new Pierce Arrow with a chauffeur who would drive her anywhere she wanted to go, but May rarely left the mansion. When she did appear in public, she made fun of her failing legs, referring to them as "pipe stems."

Al took his wife to the hot springs in Montana, and May gained a few pounds. Both she and Al knew she was living on borrowed time. May had tried all the remedies, seen all the doctors, and nothing had helped. It was time to decide what they would do with their vast fortune. May signed everything over to her husband, knowing he would follow her wishes. Both of the Huttons loved children, and since they had not been blessed with a child of their own, they decided their estate would go toward helping orphans.

On October 6, 1915, at the age of 55, May Arkwright Hutton passed away in her sleep. Her big, vigorous body and large heart had finally given up. The woman who had once claimed, "The Lord gave me the money to serve more effectively," had departed from this earth.

May's funeral was held at home. The Huttons' mansion was filled with mourners from all walks of life, who came to pay their last respects to a lady they would never forget. May was buried at Fairmount Cemetery in Spokane, on a cliff overlooking the Spokane River, with her suffragist friends in attendance. As the coffin was lowered into the ground, the president of the State Women's Democratic Club kneeled down to a basket at her feet and released a white dove — May would have been pleased.

After his wife's death, Al set out to fulfill her wishes. He built The Hutton Settlement, a home for orphaned children, and within the first year 80 children had a place to live. Al became known as Daddy Hutton, for this kind man gave far more than money to the home — he provided love; they were all his children.

On November 3, 1928, Levi W. "Al" Hutton joined the wife he

so dearly loved. His quiet funeral was held in the Masonic Temple; there were so many flowers they overflowed into the street. The silent mourners watched as their friend, "a beloved benefactor of mankind," was laid to rest beside his May.

May Arkwright Hutton

*She was a generous lady who shared her
wealth with those less fortunate.*

Courtesy of M65 Hutton Coll., L.M. 55-box 2-file-2, Northwest Museum of Arts & Culture/Eastern Washington State Historical Society, Spokane, WA.

Levi W. "Al" Hutton

He was a beloved benefactor of mankind.

A Celebration of Mrs. Duniway's Birthday

Mrs. Hutton is in the front row holding flowers at the 78th birthday of

Mrs. Abigail Scott Duniway, who is standing at the center of the picture wearing a lace cap.

Mrs. Duniway, The Grand Old Lady of Oregon

With less than a sixth-grade education, Abigail Scott Duniway became a noted journalist and prominent suffragist who gained recognition as a dedicated leader for women's rights.

She was born on October 22, 1843, in a little log cabin in Tazewell County, Illinois, the daughter of Ann and John Tucker Scott. The Scotts were a farming family who had wished for a son, and considered the birth of a girl "almost too grievous to be borne."

During her early years, the family suffered floods, drought, short crops and an abundance of insects. Abigail grew into a frail, skinny little girl who knew the meaning of the word chores. As she watched her overworked, sickly mother bear nine children, one after the other, the girl decided she would not live that kind of life.

At the age of 16, when Abigail first heard about women's rights and suffrage, it changed her life. From that day forward, she vowed to help the women of America fight for the right to vote.

In 1851, Tucker Scott decided to move his family to Oregon. Although his wife did not want to go, she had no choice. During the terrible journey, Abigail watched both her mother and little brother die on the trail. When the Scotts arrived in Oregon they were ragged, poor, and weary. Mr. Scott soon remarried a younger woman.

At the age of 18, Abigail married Benjamin C. Duniway, a gentle man who would not impose his will upon a wife. Although the couple had seven children, Mrs. Duniway managed to write a novel, as well as columns for several newspapers. She also joined suffragists Susan B. Anthony and Elizabeth Cady Stanton and helped them lecture in the West. It was during this time that May Arkwright Hutton met Abigail and joined the ladies in their fight for women's rights.

Mrs. Duniway fought a 42-year battle to achieve her goal, and in 1912, she became the first woman in Oregon to register at a national election. Due to her tireless efforts, Oregon became the seventh state to allow women the right to vote.

— Excerpted from *High-Spirited Women of the West,*
by Anne Seagraves

Riding the Rails

Al is standing at the left with May seated
below with her lady friends.

May Arkwright Goes to the Baltimore Convention

"May Arkwright Hutton carries the Spokane County endorsement for delegate to the national convention in Baltimore. Now, in the county convention were numerous male democrats who never believed in women meddling with politics to anything like the extent of going to a national convention in official capacity. They would be just as comfortable with women absent from county conventions such as caucuses and primaries.

Only One Woman a Veteran in Politics
Mrs. Hutton has served as both county and state delegate in Idaho and she ran for the legislature once there. She was defeated but the only democrats elected down there that year were constable and justice of the peace.

She began to absorb politics at the age of 10, when it became her duty to read to her grandfather who had lost his eyesight, but not his keen interest in politics. As to her chance for the national delegation from this state she says she is in the hands of the convention and that she hopes that other women will be recognized in the power and interest that they now hold in this state."

— Taken from an article in May Arkwright Hutton's scrapbook, from the *Spokesman Review*, no date was recorded.

May's grandfather once told her the following: "Hitch your wagon to a star girlie. You may never achieve the eminence to which you aspire, but place no limit on your aspirations. . . ."

May had no fear of anyone with social status or wealth; she took the advice of her grandfather and became a very powerful lady.

Working the Hercules
May is at the left with three unidentified women;
all are wearing overalls.

The Famous Hercules Mine

The mine was a real "Glory Hole," and many believed
it to be the richest silver ore ever found.

Courtesy of County of Inyo, Eastern California Museum

Dr. Nellie MacKnight Doyle

Chapter 7

NELLIE MACKNIGHT DOYLE
THE BELOVED LADY DOCTOR OF OWENS VALLEY

I n 1875, a professor of medicine wrote: "Female doctors are failures. It is a fact that there are six to eight ounces less brain matter in the female, which shows how handicapped she is." With those words echoing in her head, Nellie MacKnight, at the age of 17, entered Toland Hall in San Francisco to study medicine. Three years later she walked out with a diploma in her hand, and spent the rest of her life serving humanity.

Nellie MacKnight Doyle was born December 15 1873, to Smith and Olive MacKnight in Petrolia, Pennsylvania. Her father was a surveyor and her mother a gentle homemaker.

Although they lived in a comfortable home, Smith MacKnight was not happy. He felt there were few opportunities left in Pennsylvania for a man of his profession, and, like many men of that era, he wanted to go to California to find his fortune. As Nellie's mother, Olive, listened to her husband's talk of moving West, she was filled with apprehension. Olive was a small, subdued woman who always accepted her husband's demands without complaint, but she had no desire to leave her orderly life.

When Nellie was five, her father made an abrupt decision to fulfill his dream. He was moving West, and he was going alone. His wife was never asked for her opinion, but was simply told she had to leave her home and move in with her husband's people near the small town of Madrid, New York. She watched in alarm as her house and priceless belongings were sold; it would do no good to protest.

Smith MacKnight kissed his wife and daughter good-bye with a promise to send for them soon. With a heavy heart, Olive took Nellie's small hand and they dutifully left for New York. Mrs.

MacKnight was a little woman with beautiful, thick dark hair and smooth white hands. She was a skilled seamstress and made all of the family's clothing, always creating exquisite dresses for Nellie. Now they were both on their way to an unknown future to live with people they had never met.

In her autobiography, *A Child Goes Forth*, Nellie described the few years she spent at her grandmother's farm as happy ones. Her father's brothers, Alex and George, were kind, and she adored her cheerful, rosy-cheeked grandmother who made both her mother and her feel welcome.

Life in the old farmhouse was busy and new to Nellie. There were animals to pet, butter to churn, and wonderful meals that turned Nellie into a plump little girl. Her mother kept her dressed in clean, beautiful dresses and every day she carefully curled Nellie's long hair. Olive wanted her daughter to grow up to be a beautiful, proud woman.

Those were good years for Nellie. They went ice-skating on the frozen ponds in the winter and swimming in the creek during the summer. The old farm was filled with the child's happy laughter. Then one day, it all came to an end when Nellie's beloved grandmother became ill. The family listened in fear as the doctor told them that Grandma MacKnight had the dreaded typhoid fever. No one knew at that time how she caught it, but years later Nellie learned it was from the drinking water, which was supplied by a cistern on the roof. When her grandmother died, Nellie and her mother were asked to leave the farm. Her uncle Alex was marrying a sophisticated lady who didn't want them living with her. So again the mother and daughter were forced to pack their belongings and begin a new life; as usual Smith MacKnight wrote his wife that he didn't have any money to send. They were on their own.

Unfortunately, their new home was not to be a happy one. Olive took her daughter to Bridgeport, Connecticut, where she found employment in a corset factory and became just another overworked "stitcher." The lovely lady with her soft hands worked feverishly on a large machine, turning out as many corsets as she could to support herself and her daughter. Nellie continued her education, and after school she joined her mother at the factory where she earned a few pennies a day folding pieces of coarse material. It was hard work for the eight-year-old child who had to wear a thimble to protect her finger.

Nellie's mother had always been a respected woman and she didn't want anyone to know how desperately poor they had become. She rented a small two-room apartment in the attic of a building in a good neighborhood, for the lady wanted Nellie to have a decent address and go to a fine school. They ate the cheapest food available, and no matter how weary Olive was, she kept her daughter dressed in beautiful clothes and continued to curl her hair. She prayed nightly for a letter from her husband telling her they could join him in California, but that letter never arrived.

One day Olive caught her hand in a machine and it became infected. She kept on working, however, so she could take care of Nellie. Finally, the pain in her hand and despair over her husband's lack of interest in their well being became too much for the gentle lady; she ended her own life by taking an overdose of laudanum. Before she died Olive asked Nellie to forgive her.

Nellie's uncle Alex came to take her back to the farm, but the once happy home had disappeared; it was no longer a place of warmth and comfort. Uncle Alex had let the farm run down and his wife, Sade, was not interested in cleaning the house. She had a new baby and she hated housework. The only good thing she saw in Nellie's living with them was that the child was young and strong. From the day she arrived, Nellie took over full responsibility of the baby and the house. The nine-year-old girl eagerly went to work, for she wanted desperately to make Sade love her.

Nellie wrote her father faithfully, always asking him to let her move to California, and his reply was always the same, "Not yet. Be a good girl and study hard in school." She never told him how hard her life was, nor that she had outgrown her clothing. Nellie did study hard, but she had no time for friends. She rushed home from school to care for the baby and the housework, always hoping that someday Sade would say a kind word or show a little affection. Once in a while the woman would make Nellie a new dress out of cheap material that never fit her properly. It was as though she wanted to make the child as ugly as she could so other people would dislike her. Nellie's once beautiful curls were replaced by clumsy braids, and she lived in a continual state of drudgery.

During those terrible years, Nellie corresponded with her mother's dearest friend, a lady she called "Aunt" Mary. Mary would reply with letters of love for the child. Then one day Nellie's whole life exploded. Sade called her a name that she knew was bad, and at that point the girl gave up all hope of being loved. Nellie left the next day and did not return to the farm. She walked four miles to Aunt Mary's home where she was welcomed with open arms — Nellie never again saw her uncle Alex or Sade.

Nellie remained with Aunt Mary, against her father's wishes, for the next two years. When Mary's family moved to the Dakota Territory, Nellie went with them. Her life with that wonderful family, who had very little money, was a happy one. Mary made pretty dresses for the girl's maturing body and Nellie grew tall and strong. For the first time in her life, people said she was pretty.

When she was 14, Nellie's father sent for her to join him in California. She packed her things and said a tearful good-bye to Aunt Mary and the family that had been like her own. Nellie boarded the train filled with apprehension, for she barely remembered the man who was her father; it was as though she was on her way to meet a stranger.

When the train reached Reno, Nevada, Smith MacKnight was at the station to meet his daughter; no doubt he was just as nervous as Nellie. Although her father's face was covered with a beard and he was wearing a plaid shirt, Nellie recognized him. Smith took his daughter in his arms and together they left for the beautiful Owens Valley of California. They would make their home in the small community of Bishop. Nellie knew she would always miss her mother and Aunt Mary, but at that moment, after nine years of waiting, she must have finally felt safe and loved.

The sprawling Owens Valley was different from the farm in New York and the harshness of the Dakotas. There was an abundance of water, and rich cultivated fields of alfalfa, grain, and corn covered the landscape. The whole valley was surrounded by the majestic Sierra Nevada Mountains. In Bishop she found that farms were called ranches, farmers were ranchers, and most homes were made of adobe. Cowboys swaggered along the streets, which were real streets, and everyone turned out to welcome the daughter of Smith MacKnight. He was once again a surveyor as well as a respected member of the community.

Nellie boarded and attended school at the Inyo Academy, where the teachers were excellent and her classmates friendly. Since Smith was away most of the time, many of Nellie's holidays were spent at the ranches of her friends. She learned the history of the people and the area from those kind families. With all her newfound happiness, however, there was still something missing for Nellie; a mother's love.

Smith MacKnight's pride in his daughter was obvious, and he soon began taking her on fishing trips. He shared with Nellie the beauty of the outdoors and taught her to survive in the wilderness. But, underneath all his show of affection, there still remained the stern, overbearing man she remembered. It was on one of those trips her father told her he was getting married again. Nellie was shocked, and he made excuses, assuring her she would have a real home with a woman who was both good and kind. Nellie remembered the letters he wrote filled with promises and her mother's words, "Till Poppa sends for us." The girl was crushed and once more she felt alone.

Nellie returned to school, and buried herself in studies. When Smith and his new wife came home from their honeymoon, they moved into a house across the street from the Academy and Nellie moved in with them. She soon realized there was no reason to fear her stepmother, for they were both under the rigid control of her now violent, suspicious, and unreasonable father. He wouldn't let Nellie accept invitations to attend hayrides or country dances; a date with a boy was out of the question. She found herself a prisoner in her own home and school became Nellie's only escape. Although Nellie's stepmother often tried to interfere, she received only hostile silence from her husband, who never let go of his possessive hold on his daughter. The two women learned to lean on each other and they endured Smith's tyrannical rages in silence.

At the age of 17, Nellie graduated from the Academy; she was valedictorian of her class and had a burning desire to become an author. Her father, however, had other plans. If his daughter intended to further her education, she had two choices: law or medicine — it was up to her. In her autobiography, Nellie wrote that when she thought of her grandmother's terrible death from typhoid fever and her mother's painful infection, she decided to become a doctor.

Although Nellie was anxious to escape her dominant father, Smith MacKnight insisted upon escorting her to San Francisco. When Nellie saw how large the city was, she was glad he had. There were masses of strange people, large buildings, and fast moving vehicles everywhere. It was totally confusing for the young woman from the small town of Bishop. She clung tightly to her father's arm as they made their way down a bustling street to find lodging for the night.

The next few days were busy. They visited Toland Hall, where

Nellie would be one of three women in a class of about 100 students. Her father remained with her until they found a "proper" lodging house. When it was time for Smith to leave, Nellie went with him to catch the ferry, and as she said good-bye, she realized that, in spite of his terrible temperament, he did love her. She waved until he was out of sight, and then returned to her boarding house with a lump in her throat.

Nellie was on her own for the first time. She was to enter a school that had a reputation of making a woman as uncomfortable as possible. The following story clearly illustrates what Nellie was facing:

In 1873, Lucy Wanzer, who was the first woman to receive a degree in medicine in California, applied for admission to Toland Hall. She was firmly told that a medical lecture hall, a dissecting room and clinics were not proper places for women, and advised to go East to study. Although the school reluctantly accepted Lucy, they also made life miserable for her. However, they had not realized how spirited the woman was; she had an answer for everything. When a professor stated that if a woman wanted to study medicine she should first have her ovaries removed, Lucy quietly replied, if that is true, then men students should have their testicles removed. When Lucy received her medical degree, she became a beacon of indomitable courage for those women who followed in her footsteps.

As Nellie walked into Toland Hall, she thought of Lucy Wanzer, and entered her first class determined to be as successful as that young woman had been.

Nellie had three months to demonstrate whether she was capable to enroll in the regular term of medicine. The first day in the dissection room was the hardest; she nearly fainted. But when Nellie looked around, she saw that the sight and smell of rotting bodies made even the strongest male student appear weak; she lived through it. That night on her way home, the young woman took deep breaths of the fresh sea air to cleanse her lungs of the clinging odor of death.

From that day forward, Nellie worked industriously, many times falling asleep with the book *Gray's Anatomy* held to her breast. She was confused by the strange words and she struggled through the maze of new terminology. The other two women were older than Nellie, and had both been teachers before the new women's movement spurred them on to greater things. They lived separate lives and although the women were polite, it was clear they had no desire to become friends. So Nellie struggled on alone with the feeling she was just another annoyance to her professors as well as the other female students.

Most of the teachers resented the women and were rude to them. A few took great pleasure in telling ribald jokes that Nellie didn't understand. The quizmaster was the hardest to work with. He was a young man who resented the intrusion of women in what he considered a male profession. This man never failed to make school miserable for Nellie; it was as though he had sought her out. She would hide her tears and bite her tongue rather than let him see how he upset her, and she passed his quizzes with flying colors.

As Nellie wrote progress letters to her father, she must have let some of her unhappiness creep in, for he became angry. Smith MacKnight could not tolerate failure in anyone, especially his own daughter. Something like that would reflect against him and cause his pride to suffer. Rather than face disgrace, he offered to let Nellie leave medical school and attend regular classes at the University at Berkeley. But Nellie had no desire to change schools. She found medicine a challenge and had developed an intense desire to become a doctor more than anything else in the world. By that time she had passed her first year and was eager to continue on. Besides, Nellie had learned to live with the rude remarks and the obscene jokes; they no longer embarrassed her.

As Nellie began her second year, she encountered Dr. Cole of obstetrics and gynecology. He was a man who delighted in tormenting female students. He felt they were doomed to failure and should return to their homes. Despite that, Dr. Cole was a brilliant surgeon and Nellie learned many valuable lessons from him. She never forgot Dr. Cole or the things he taught about childbirth and the medical problems of women — they were a great help to her in later years.

By the time Nellie was in her last year of medical school, she was one of the group. The male students accepted her and she was invited to accompany them as they explored the many exciting places in San Francisco. Nellie had only two regrets: she didn't have any women friends and was still forced to dress in shabby, unsuitable clothing. Her father selected her dresses and she wore them. Smith MacKnight liked material with large checks, and Nellie, who weighed 175 pounds, always felt like she resembled a large mountain. In spite of her size and uncomplimentary dresses, Nellie never lacked for escorts or admirers.

As graduation approached, Nellie passed the final examinations without a problem. She had conquered medical school and was looking forward to graduation. Before that day, however, Nellie was called to the Dean's office. As she stood beside his desk, fully convinced he was going to tell her she failed, the Dean asked her what name she wanted on her diploma, surely not Nellie! He said Nellie was too common, she needed something more dignified. So Nellie re-christened herself "Helen" and that is the name that went on her diploma as well as her first "shingle," although she was still called Nellie.

Nellie had decided to take a year of internship before returning to Bishop. Her father, as usual, had other plans. Suspicious of her desire to remain in San Francisco, he felt there had to be an ulterior motive. She must come home now, and help him pay off the money he had been forced to borrow for her. Nellie was terrified, nevertheless, she held her ground. She would accept the internship and somehow live off the pittance it paid. When her father left he was furious, for he knew his daughter was no longer completely under his control.

Before he returned to Bishop, however, Smith attended the graduation, and it gave him the pride he needed. His daughter was beautiful in her new black dress and the cap upon her pompadour looked special. When her name was read, Nellie felt a new dignity as she walked up the aisle to receive her diploma. The little girl from the small farm in New York, the corset factory in Connecticut, and the Dakota Territory had become a woman doctor. When Dr. MacKnight was handed her diploma, she no doubt felt the spirit of those who had gone before her and the power of those who would follow.

With three years of medical school behind her, Dr. MacKnight was ready to begin her internship. She knew it would be hard for a woman, since men were becoming frantic as they watched females invade their sacred world.

Women doctors were not generally allowed to practice at the local hospitals, but Nellie had secured a position at the new children's hospital. The facility had been founded by a group of women physicians in defiance of the mores society had forced upon them. Nellie was inspired by their bravery. In those women she found the banner of a bright future that would someday ignore prejudice and concentrate instead upon caring for the ill.

As Nellie began her internship, she had no idea how valuable the training would be in her future. One of the Children's Hospital's original founders, Charlotte Brown, M.D., managed to gather enough money to erect the small building. In 1890, it was expanded to include maternity care, something few women of that era received. Although the hospital had only 20 beds, an amazing number of women and children received competent care. There were three women physicians: a resident, an assistant, and Dr. MacKnight. The other women who had attended the medical school with Nellie went directly into private practice.

In her autobiography, Nellie wrote she would never be able to express her gratitude for the opportunity of the practical experience Children's Hospital made available. Had she gone into private practice without the knowledge she gained there, Nellie feared she would have made many mistakes. The hospital's maternity ward was above reproach. The good women of San Francisco saw to that. There were free beds for the unemployed, but sadly there was no place for a fatherless child to be born. However, a woman in distress ended that. When she was denied a bed, the mother went out and gave birth to her baby in the courtyard. Her cries were so loud that everyone ran to assist. Later, it was said the mother and child were convalescing none the worse for their experience.

Nellie learned to change dressings, an experience that was painful to her. Many of the children suffered from open sores which led to diseased bone that had to be cleaned and packed daily. Since there were no anesthetics the children were in great pain. It took all of Nellie's strength to do her job with the little sufferers who pleaded, "Don't, Doctor, please Doctor." After she finished, however, the smiles of relief they gave her made it a rewarding experience. Even though she weighed 175 pounds, Nellie became known as the "Little Doctor," because of her gentleness with the small ones.

While at the hospital, Dr. MacKnight assisted in amputations on private patients. The first surgical procedure was one of the hardest things she ever had to do. For one terrifying instant she thought she could not make that first incision. With her teeth clenched and the scalpel clutched in her hand, she finally did it, and was soon absorbed in the operation, forgetting her fears.

During her internship, Nellie traveled with other doctors throughout the city making calls. They visited clinics as well as homes, doing all they could for the injured and ill. Out of those visits grew one of Nellie's many causes. She developed a burning desire to help build a ward for the incurable — there were so many pitiful children in need of love and comfort during their last days. As she appealed for help, a warm-hearted newspaperwoman began to share stories of the children who were turned away. Her articles started the first funds that helped to build the "Little Jim" ward.

As other women graduates entered the hospital, Dr. MacKnight was transferred to the maternity ward, where new experiences awaited her. Nellie was thrilled to learn so much while helping so many.

Her learning experience came to an end when Smith MacKnight told Nellie she had to return to Bishop. Her stepmother was very ill and the local doctors had given up hope. Although her heart sank at the thought of leaving Children's Hospital, Nellie knew the needs of that plain, patient woman, who had been so good to her, could not be denied. Dr. MacKnight was 21 and ready to go into private practice. She said good-bye to her friends and colleagues and the "Little Doctor" left immediately. The only fear Nellie had was her father's influence over her life.

When she arrived home Nellie found her stepmother needed nursing and tenderness more than prescriptions. There were two other physicians in Bishop: one was an old army doctor, who refused to consult with her, and the other was a young man, who treated a woman doctor as a joke. Under Dr. MacKnight's careful care, her stepmother began to improve and eventually recovered. It wasn't long before everybody in Bishop knew about it and the news spread throughout the rest of the sprawling valley.

Nellie's first office was the front room of her father's house. She purchased a small amount of drugs, for she would make her own prescriptions, and proudly hung her shingle: "Helen MacKnight, M.D., Physician and Surgeon." That shingle was the first of many conflicts with Smith. He was outraged because he had christened his daughter Nellie, not Helen — the name on the shingle, however, was not changed.

In order to have transportation, Nellie bought a small buggy with a jump seat and two horses. She harnessed (and unharnessed) the horses herself, then climbed into the buggy, took the reins, and away she would go. That little buggy traveled all over the valley in every kind of weather; no one was ever denied her care.

When a message arrived summoning Nellie to a mining camp 150 miles away, she packed her medical bag, took a train to a small town, and then rode a buckboard the rest of the way. When she arrived at the barren camp, she found her patient was the superintendent of the mine, and he was very ill with the dreaded typhoid. On the floor, by his side, his Indian wife sat waiting with worry written all over her face. She had the cabin spotlessly clean and her love for the man was evident. With the memory of her grandmother in her mind, Nellie struggled to help the patient survive. After a week long battle with death, the man began to recover and Nellie was able to return home; she knew his wife would provide the care he needed.

When she arrived home, the townspeople were already aware that Dr. MacKnight had saved the superintendent from typhoid, and Nellie was no longer looked upon as a "last resort" physician. She soon became known as "Dr. Nellie."

The next few weeks were unbearable for the family. Her father had decided to retire and live off his investment: Nellie. From then on he observed every move she made. He began questioning any male patient who came to her office and watched to see how long he stayed. Smith even forced his daughter to ask some patients to leave. It seemed Nellie couldn't win; she had to get away from his fanatical possession of her.

When a check for $100 arrived from the superintendent whom she had saved from typhoid, Nellie rented a room on Main Street and opened a new office. It was then Smith MacKnight realized his daughter had finally moved out on her own. He went into a rage that lasted all night and then deserted his wife to dig for gold south of town, leaving her penniless. Dr. MacKnight set her stepmother up in a small business of her own, something the lady had always wanted. Years later, when her father's health began to fail, Nellie made his last days as comfortable as she could; Smith MacKnight was paid in full!

As Dr. MacKnight's reputation spread, the chronically ill patients who had visited her only in desperation were joined by people from all walks of life. Nellie delivered babies and cared for children and women with special needs. Her practice flourished and Nellie was able to relax and make friends.

One day Nellie met a young doctor, Guy Doyle, who was trying his luck mining at Mammoth Lakes. He was a handsome man with enough vitality to fill a whole room. Within a few weeks the doctors were keeping company; they had so much in common. There was one problem, however; Nellie had seen what gold fever could do to people. She remembered her helpless little mother and the tragedy of her life. Whenever Dr. Doyle talked about their future, Nellie would change the subject, for she could never marry a man who depended upon a gold strike to support his family.

One day Guy came to her office excited over a "find." When it turned out to be just another dream, Dr. Doyle decided to leave mining to others and resume his medical practice. Nellie rejoiced in secret over his loss, for now she could look ahead to a future with the man with whom she had fallen in love.

Dr. Doyle opened his practice, and Nellie wrote in her autobiography that they had an old-fashioned horse and buggy courtship. On a beautiful day in June, the two were wed. Nellie wore a crisp, white organdy gown with ruffles that touched the floor. Their wedding was small, but that night hundreds of people turned out for a real old-time Western chivaree to celebrate the marriage of their own Dr. Nellie.

During the next several years the couple worked tirelessly in the expanding community. They added a team of fast horses and a double buggy. When Nellie was expecting her first child, that didn't hold her down. She went into the country to deliver a baby three weeks before the birth of her own daughter, and another baby three weeks after. When she was needed, Dr. MacKnight Doyle would wrap her child in a blanket and take her along.

The doctors continued to practice in the Owens Valley until World War I, when Dr. Doyle answered the call. He might have been a bit gray around the temples, but he was ready to serve the country he loved. Dr. Doyle became part of the Medical Corps and was stationed in New York. Nellie and their two children, for she had also given birth to a son, left Bishop to be near their husband and father. She had practiced medicine in the valley for over 21 years, and her friends and patients hated to see their beloved Dr. Nellie leave.

When the war ended, the Doyles settled in the Berkeley Hills, across the bay from the city that had been so special to Nellie in her youth. Dr. Doyle became an eye, nose, and throat specialist, and Nellie practiced anesthetics at the University of California Hospital. Along with her hospital work, she began writing short stories, and in 1934, Nellie received the Commonwealth Award for her autobiography, *A Child Went Forth.*

After a long life of service, Dr. Nellie MacKnight Doyle passed away in 1956 at the St. Francis Hospital in San Francisco. She was a remarkable woman who overcame her unhappy childhood, and had the courage to study medicine at a time when lady doctors were frowned upon. During her long life, Dr. Nellie cared for the ill and helped to open the door so other women could follow.

The story of Dr. Nellie has been made possible through the courtesy of Genny Smith Books, the publisher of Dr. Nellie. *Although the book is out of print at this time, a new edition is forthcoming.*

Nellie MacKnight

During her final year at the Inyo Academy

Dr. Nellie MacKnight Doyle
She was affectionately called "Dr. Nellie."

Courtesy of The Deschutes County Historical Society

Kathleen Rockwell

Chapter 8

KATHLEEN ROCKWELL
A LEGENDARY LADY

She rolled her own cigarettes, drank whiskey from a flask, and loved publicity. During her colorful life, Kathleen "Kate" Rockwell raised more than one eyebrow with her outrageous antics, while capturing the hearts of others for her generosity to those in need.

Kathleen Eloisa Rockwell was born in Junction City, Kansas, in 1876. Her father, John Rockwell, was a railroad man and her mother, Martha Murphy, a waitress. Kathleen was a celebrity at birth, for she was a centennial baby.

When Kathleen was three months old, her father was transferred to Oswego, Kansas, and took his family with him. While there, Mrs. Rockwell ran the restaurant at the train station. Three years later, she divorced her husband and married Francis Bettis, the prominent attorney who had handled the proceedings. Within a year they moved, with little Kathleen, to Spokane Falls, which at that time was a fledgling community in eastern Washington State.

Mr. Bettis was a very wealthy man who wanted to give both his wife and stepdaughter the best of everything. They moved into one of the largest and finest homes in the city. Kathleen had her own governess and her mother had a personal maid. Her stepfather adored the child and showered her with gifts; anything little "Kitty" wanted, she was given. Although Kitty thrived in the limelight and enjoyed her new lifestyle, her mother found it hard to adjust. She was a simple woman who was not used to having a large home with servants. The constant entertaining her husband expected was often more than she could handle.

Kitty learned from her doting stepfather how to manipulate

people and get the best out of every situation; she was a very perceptive child. As Kitty grew older, she became an outspoken girl who danced her way through childhood, charming everyone with whom she came in contact. Her parents tried to teach the effervescent child to become a lady, but she was born to be a hoyden. Kitty found attending school boring, and would run off to play with her many friends as soon as an opportunity arose. She had a deep love of nature and a natural ability to dance. Whenever Kitty heard music, her feet took on a life of their own, and she would whirl gracefully about the room to the rhythm from the victrola.

In desperation, her parents entered Kitty at St. Joseph's Academy in St. Paul, Minnesota, but the girl wouldn't have any part of it. Although she learned her lessons, the spirited Kitty constantly created mischief. The nuns finally shipped the wayward child back to her parents. The couple tried two other schools, and each time Kitty came home in what they considered disgrace.

After her return to Spokane, Kitty discovered boys and parties, and a new set of problems began. While the young woman was busy creating havoc, her stepfather lost his fortune in the stock market. When his seemingly endless supply of money abruptly disappeared, Mrs. Bettis divorced him. She took the proceeds of their home and moved herself and Kitty to New York, in hopes of starting a new life.

Kitty always loved anything new, so she happily left Spokane with dreams of achieving success in New York. She felt the city, with its bright lights and large theatres, would surely appreciate her dancing ability. Unfortunately, her mother ran out of what little money she had, and Kitty, for the first time in her life, realized she would have to go to work.

Mrs. Bettis found a small apartment and a job in a shirt factory, working for four dollars a week. When Kitty started her search for employment, she found it a bit harder. She was a beautiful young woman, and it appeared her prospective employers were more interested in getting a little more from her than a day's work. After a few weeks of fighting off lecherous men, Kitty became desperate. She was only 16, but Kitty knew she had to find something when she saw an ad in the newspaper, "Chorus girls wanted. No experience." Kitty answered the ad and was immediately hired; she would be making $18 a week. Her whole life changed. She would be paid more than her mother for doing what she enjoyed.

Kitty's natural talent and her long shapely legs were a great attraction. She easily learned the routines and within a few weeks had top billing. Since the name Kitty did not sound professional, she began calling herself Kate. Although Mrs. Bettis was upset over her daughter's dancing career, Kate refused to leave the chorus. At that point, Martha surrendered all hopes of her daughter becoming a lady.

While Kate performed in small variety houses, women like Lillian Russell and Zeigfeld's Anna Held, were becoming famous. Those entertainers set the styles; whatever they wore, the women copied. Kate, as all the chorus girls, read about the beautiful stars and dreamed of the day when she too would become popular. That, however, was not to be. Kate never became famous on Broadway; her fame was found in the frozen ice of the Yukon.

When a friend wrote there were plenty of good paying jobs for dancers in Spokane, Kate decided to return home. She contacted what she thought was a reputable theatre, and signed a contract. Her mother would have to remain in New York until Kate could send for her.

In Spokane, the "reputable" theatre turned out to be a saloon with a small stage in the corner. On the first night, Kate received a small record book and was told that a bell would summon her to a box where a gentleman was waiting for her to join him in a drink — but she didn't drink!

Kate was only 17 and too frightened to walk out on her contract, so she stayed. At the end of the evening, she realized all the men wanted was someone to talk to, and the money was more than she ever imagined. So Kate remained, and became a percentage girl, pushing drinks for a kickback on every one she sold. The only problem was that Kate could never hang on to money; she spent it almost as fast as she earned it. There was always someone who needed a loan or was down on their luck, so it was several months before she could send for her mother.

When the big gold strike hit the Yukon Territory, Kate, along with most of the entertainers, wanted a share of the riches. She was getting bored with her job anyway. When the opportunity to become part of the large Savoy Theatrical Company came along, Kate grabbed it. By that time she had developed a low, throaty voice and could sing almost as well as she could dance. Kate signed on as one of the headliners, and was soon on her way to the wild, freewheeling town of Dawson, Alaska. Made up of tents, shacks, and rough buildings, its focal point was a street filled with saloons, gambling houses, and brightly lighted theatres; it was there Kate would become known as

"Klondike Kate," and one of the first pin-up girls in the Northwest.

Working at the Savoy Theatre meant hustling drinks as well as dancing in brief, fancy costumes. Kate was young and beautiful, and from the moment she stepped upon the stage she held the audience spellbound. Her low, sexy voice, golden-red hair, and high-kicking legs created so much excitement that the sourdoughs would pound the tables. They covered the stage with gold nuggets and yelled for more, and she happily gave them encore after encore.

Following the show, the girls worked the floor, selling champagne at $15 a bottle, and dancing with the men for one dollar a minute. At first Kate was nervous when she saw so many bearded, noisy males, but she soon realized they only wanted a little bit of her time and friendship. She relaxed and became the most popular entertainer in Dawson. Kate was not like the other girls, however; she cared about the miners for themselves, not their gold. Although it has been said that Kate earned as much as $30,000 a year, she never became rich. She was always ready to grubstake a miner or help anyone down on his luck. Many times, Kate would carry a pot of soup to some poor soul's hovel, so he wouldn't starve to death.

Although there is no doubt Kate had her share of propositions, she never became a prostitute — nor was she absolutely pure. Kate had too much pride to sell herself; she was happy just to be a friend and make people feel special. The men claimed she had a heart of gold, and most were in love with her; meanwhile, the lovely dancer continued earning a fine wage.

There was no love in Kate's life until a new waiter started working at the Savoy. His name was Alexander Pantages, and although she was not aware of it at the time, he would someday break her heart as well as her bank account.

Pantages was a little taller than Kate, with deep, brooding eyes and thick, dark hair that was slicked back with oil. Some found his well-muscled body and Greek accent attractive; Kate found them delightful. Within a few weeks, she was madly in love with the illiterate waiter. It wasn't long before she was dressing him in silk shirts, and supplying the fancy cigars he liked. Pantages didn't drink, or the lovely dancer would have provided him with the best champagne available. He did, however, take an interest in the entertainment business. Pantages watched as the sourdoughs put down their sacks of gold for a bit of amusement; he was not a stupid man, but he definitely didn't have any money.

The first Christmas Eve in Dawson was a special one. The men were in high spirits and ready to celebrate, all except Johnny Matson. He had fought his way from his small cabin, through 60 miles of frozen land, to celebrate the Yuletide. Johnny wasn't tall or muscular; he was a shy Scandinavian with a heavy accent who didn't belong in a rowdy place like the Savoy. The man didn't drink, smoke, or gamble, but it was Christmas Eve and he didn't want to be alone. While Johnny sat silently watching the noisy crowd, the most beautiful female he had ever seen burst upon the stage, and everyone quieted down. The woman was Kate, dressed in an exquisite glittering costume. As she danced, she began swirling several yards of red chiffon around her body. The young Scandinavian sat mesmerized, his eyes riveted upon the stage. His gaze was so intent that Kate felt him looking at her. When she finished the number, the strange man had already left the theatre. Before leaving, however, Johnny found out her name, and he never forgot the woman called Klondike Kate. Johnny would make his way to the Savoy several times during the following year.

That night there were many lonely miners who dreamed of Kate as they huddled in their snow-drifted cabins. They wished to find a rich mine and become wealthy enough to ask Kate to marry them. But the girl had eyes for only one, the unknown Greek who served drinks, while she became famous.

As the sourdoughs thought about the girl of their dreams, Pantages dreamed about becoming king of the vaudeville circuit. However, that would take more money than he had. The fulfillment of Pantages's desires depended upon Kate Rockwell. In her, he saw his future. And, in 1903, she agreed to give him her hard-earned savings in exchange for partnership in his venture. Kate felt her lover had the rare gift of knowing how to please the public, and she was right. The man was a genius at putting together successful shows. Kate put all her love and trust into Pantages, and he promised to marry her.

After several losses in Dawson, Pantages and Kate decided to go on to Seattle, where they opened the Crystal Theatre. When their money was low, Kate went on the road and sent all her earnings to Pantages, keeping only enough for the bare necessities. The more money she mailed to him, the more he seemed to love her; Pantages was becoming a huge success. One year later, the still single Kate received a letter with a message that Alexander Pantages had married a young violinist — and the popular Kate Rockwell collapsed.

Later, she filed a breach of promise suit, but only received $5,000. Their story made headlines throughout the West, and although Kate loved publicity, this type of coverage made her look like a lovesick fool.

Heart-broken and despondent, Kate returned to what she knew best — the theatre. Her name began to appear on marquees from Los Angeles to Seattle. She danced and sang, but her feet weren't as nimble and her kicks were not as high. When she sang a love song, her voice brought tears to many eyes. Kate knew she couldn't go on performing like that. The audiences expected a lively, saucy act and she was a disappointment, for the face of Pantages was constantly in her mind.

Finally, Kate just walked away from it all. Years later, in an interview, she said she remembered a verse the old sourdoughs used to recite, "When your heart is breaking, mush on and smile," and that is what she did.

Kate went to Seattle, where her mother was selling real estate, and poured out her problems. Then she bought a horse, a six-shooter, and camping gear. Although many parts of the Northwest were still considered wild and lawless, Kate wasn't afraid, for she had already been hurt.

She headed out alone, wandering aimlessly through Washington State, pushing on to the Columbia River and eventually Central Oregon. Sometimes she stayed in a hotel, but most of the time she slept on the ground. The fresh, clean air and the beauty of the land refreshed her. In one of her many interviews, Kate claimed she fell in love with the high desert around Bend, Oregon, and called it "the surgeon of my soul." The bitterness in her heart melted away and everything seemed good again. The high desert was where she wanted to be, but at that time it was the theatre that called, and she returned to the "boards."

She unpacked her costumes and joined a vaudeville troupe, and for a while it was wonderful. Kate's mind, however, was still in Oregon. When her mother called to tell her there was a homestead for sale near Bend, Kate bought it sight unseen. She was so eager to leave, she dropped everything and said a quick good-bye. Her friends thought Kate had lost her mind. They told her she wouldn't last three months, but they were wrong — she hung on the rest of her life.

Kate bought an old wagon and a couple of horses. She had about $3,500, her diamonds, and trunks filled with fancy costumes. As she left, the dancer was filled with anticipation. That, however, quickly turned to despair when she saw what was to be her home. It stood on the high desert, forty miles from Bend, amidst miles upon miles of sagebrush and prairie. The house was a broken-down 16 by 20 foot shack, and the cold desert winds forced their way through the cracks in the wall. A flimsy shed that was supposed to be a barn stood a few feet away. She found out later that water had to be hauled in by wagon twice a week. As Kate surveyed the land she had to "prove up," which consisted of 320 acres of arid desert, no one will ever know what went through her mind. Whatever it was, the lady had courage, for she unpacked a few things and moved in for the night — and she did it in style, dressed in a fancy costume and high-heeled shoes, with a feathered hat upon her head.

The next day, the small town got their first look at the new neighbor. She arrived decked out in her best dance hall attire, as though it was opening night on Broadway. The "good" housewives looked knowingly at each other, the men hid smiles behind their hands, and the colorful lady went on about the business of shopping. She remained in Bend for the next few months while her cabin was made livable.

During that time, the citizens of Bend had a chance to get acquainted with Kate, and they had mixed opinions. Years later, in his book, *Klondike Kate,* biographer Ellis Lucia wrote, "She was controversial, beloved by some, amusing to many, and pointedly disliked by others who called her 'our destitute prostitute.'" What her neighbors thought of her made no difference to Kate. She wandered peacefully through the desert, collecting rocks, and sharing her cheerful personality with all who would take the time to talk to her. Then she left for her cabin as she had arrived, dressed to the hilt in a colorful outfit.

Kate faithfully worked her homestead. She fought the rabbits and the snowstorms, and constantly battled to clear the rocks from her land. Her attire was always the same: an old dance hall gown, high heels, and a plumed hat.

In a land that seldom yielded a crop, she wasted some of the precious water on the daisies that grew in profusion by her front door. During that time, the gossiping wives carefully watched their husbands. They knew Kate was always ready to entertain. She had invited the "boys" to drop by anytime for coffee, and many did. Soon, there was a well-worn path leading to her front door.

Kate's happiness was complete. She had replaced her love for Pantages with the solitude and quiet beauty of the land. At night, the scent of sagebrush and the lonely howl of the coyotes lulled her to sleep. Kate often attended dances at her neighbors' homes. She would go in the old buggy and whirl the night away, returning at dawn. Needless to say, she was always the most sought after dancer.

When money was scarce, Kate would go to one of the cities and earn a little cash dancing in a show. Other times she would cook, wash dishes, or even scrub a floor. While Kate was fighting for survival, Pantages was running a theatrical empire; he had everything, including wealth and power. Kate saw his theatres everywhere she went, and she knew she still loved him. Finally, in desperation, Kate went to his home in Los Angeles to ask for help. He met her at the door, handed her six dollars, and broke her heart again.

In 1929, Pantages was charged with raping a young girl. It was a scandal that rocked the whole nation. Kate was asked to testify against him in court, but she refused; she claimed she couldn't hurt him. Then she turned around and told the reporters how she had financed him and loved him, and what he had done to her in return. It made great publicity for her; the whole country was again talking about Klondike Kate. While she enjoyed the limelight, the Pantages family was devastated and his image was destroyed along with his empire. In her own way, Kate got revenge. Whether it helped to ease the pain or not, she would never say.

The Alaska-Yukon Sourdoughs held a reunion in 1931, and it wouldn't have been complete without Kate. They celebrated the old days and sang "Let Me Call You Sweetheart" to their old flame. There were stories and pictures in the newspapers, and Johnny Matson saw one of them. He had never forgotten the beautiful girl of the Yukon, so he wrote her a letter. Soon, he and Kate were writing each other. A year later, Johnny wrote Kate that he had always been in love with her, but lacked the courage to tell her. He said he knew life had not been kind to her, so he wanted to take care of her as his wife.

When Kate received his letter, she knew the shy Norwegian had always loved her. After carefully thinking it over, Kate accepted his offer. Johnny came down from the Yukon, and they met at Vancouver, B.C., to discuss it. When Kate, who was 57, said she was no longer young, Johnny looked at her with the same devotion he always had, saying it made no difference. At 70, Johnny would consider himself lucky to be married to the "Belle of the Yukon."

They were wed as soon as possible, and went to Dawson on their honeymoon, only to find it had changed like everything else. The old Savoy Theatre was in ruins, but for one brief moment, they both remembered Kate kicking her long legs and singing a simple ballad from the past; it was almost as though they could hear the music playing and the champagne corks hitting the ceiling.

Following the honeymoon, Johnny returned to his cabin; he was too old to leave now. The new Mrs. Matson went back to Oregon wearing a necklace of nuggets from her husband's claim. They saw each other every other year and exchanged letters. Johnny always sent a few nuggets and a check. Their marriage was played up in the newspapers around the nation, and everyone marveled at the strange relationship. By that time Kate had proven up her homestead and was living in Bend. She was happy, and there was plenty of publicity; everywhere she went people knew her.

Kate never stopped being active. She became an avid rock collector, traveling all over the desert in her heels, and never returning empty-handed. With the help of her friends and the volunteer fire department, a massive rock fireplace was added to her home. At that time Kate had become an honorary member of the volunteer firemen and the boys in the firehouse loved her. Whenever she heard the fire alarm, Kate would put on a huge pot of coffee, and no matter how cold it was she dashed out to join them. They could hear her old jalopy rattling down the street, and the men were grateful. Sometimes she would even share a drink from her flask with them. In return, Kate always had the privilege of riding on the fire truck during the parades, thus keeping the legend of Klondike Kate alive.

As Kate grew older, she became one of the many characters of the Old West. She often said, "I don't care if people laugh with me or at me, so long as I get a laugh." Then she would pull out her Bull Durham and papers and deftly roll a cigarette with one hand.

There was one thing missing in Kate's life — her husband. She wrote him over and over, begging him to join her in Oregon. In 1944, Johnny finally agreed. On his way to meet her, death took the mild, gentle man; his body was found frozen in one of his cabins. As Kate made arrangements for his funeral, she bravely told the media, "I guess I will just have to mush on and smile." Those were the words the newspapers carried in their many stories. The real tragedy was that Kate had really loved her Johnny.

After returning from Dawson, Kate threw herself even more

into helping others. Her home in Bend became a focal point for people of all ages. She began using her past experiences to help young people take the right path. They came to her with their problems, and she never violated their trust. Many wayward girls were provided with good advice, and left after receiving financial assistance. Kate soon became known as "Aunt Kate," a name she honored so much she claimed she would rather be Aunt Kate to Central Oregon, and the Sweetheart of the Sourdoughs, than a millionaire.

During her lifetime, Kate had made a fortune, and lost a fortune. Money was made to be spent and she knew how to spend it. At that point in life, she had sold everything but her home, and in her late sixties had to make her own way. Yet, Kate continued to give to those in need. If someone was homeless, she either found them a place to live, or shared her own home. She would beg the shopkeepers to give her their old produce and meat scraps to make soup for the hungry hobos. She always told the men they were not down and out unless they lost faith in themselves.

Kate had a couple of boarders, and one of them was destined to become her last husband. W. L. VanDuran had known Kate for years. When he lost part of his eyesight, and could no longer see clearly enough to run his accounting business, Kate helped him. It was said she raised enough money to pay for his surgery, and then nursed him back to health. In 1946, two years after Johnny Matson's death, Kate and VanDuran were married. He was 71 years old, and, although Kate claimed she was 68, she was really the same age as VanDuran. They were both anxious to be married. Following the ceremony, Kate quipped, "I didn't think I would get another chance! I was once the Flower of the North, but the petals are falling awful [sic] fast, honey."

The couple moved to Sweet Home, Oregon, where Kate lived another ten years, always lending a hand to others and looking for an opportunity to get a little publicity. In 1957, Kathleen Rockwell Matson VanDuran quietly passed away in her sleep in her home, at the age of 81. Her ashes were spread by airplane over Central Oregon, the place she finally found peace and loved so well. With her passing, the footlights went out and the curtains came down on the final act, for Kate Rockwell had left the stage.

Kate Rockwell

She was one of the last Western pioneers.

Courtesy of Manuscripts, Special Collections, University
Archives, University of Washington Libraries. #2242

Alexander Pantages

The theatre magnate who took Kate's
money and married another woman.

Courtesy of The Deschutes County Historical Society

"Klondike Kate"

She was "Queen of the Yukon."

BIBLIOGRAPHY

Primary Sources

Chapter 1. Elizabeth Smith Collins: "The Cattle Queen of Montana"
Books: *Jedediah Smith and the Opening of the West,* Morgan, Dale L. 1964. Documents: *Choteau Acantha, Teton County, a History,* 1988; *Sad the River Flows,* Erwin, Alice, 1950. Women's File, Montana Historical Society, Helena, Montana, *Montana Queens Experience as Indian Captive.* Newspapers: *Benzion News,* 1981; *Choteau Acantha,* June, 1921; *Fort Benton River Press,* April 3, 1895; *Great Falls Tribune,* 1901; *Montana Journal,* July-August, 1991; *Mountaineer, The,* 1894; *River Press,* 1895, *Seattle Post,* 1901.

Chapter 2. Emma Nevada: "The Comstock Nightingale"
Documents: California Hall of Fame, Emma Nevada, "The Comstock Nightingale." Newspapers: *Carson Free Lance,* June 1, 1885; *Las Vegas Age,* July 12, 1940. *Nevada State Journal:* June 16, 1940; June 23, 1940; June 25, 1940; June 28, 1940; June 29, 1940; November 7, 1940; September 8, 1940, September 22, 1959; February 22, 1959. *Oakland Tribune:* August 25, 1940; September 1, 1940; September 8, 1940; September 22, 1940; February 22, 1959. *Pony Express Courier,* Placerville, CA. July 7, 1940. *Reese River Reveille*: March 14, 1885; March 25, 1885; May 16, 1885; May 18, 1985; June 1, 1885; February 22, 1936.

Chapter 3. Ethel Robertson Macia: "Tombstone's Lady of the Rose"
Books: *The Lady of the Rose,* Devere, Dorothy, 1993. Newspapers: *Bisbee Review,* date unknown; *The Huachuchua Scout,* April 16, 1959; *The Phoenix Gazette,* June, 1954, August, 1961. Magazines: *The National Geographic,* 1999. The story of Ethel Robertson Macia has been made possible through the generosity of Dorothy and Burton Devere. They have spent numerous hours going through old documents, letters and family photos to provide accurate information about Ethel Macia, Burton Devere's grandmother.

Chapter 4. Ellen Craft: "A Race for Freedon"
Books: *Black Foremothers,* Sterling, Dorothy 1979; *Freedman's Book, The,* Child, Lydia, 1968; *Notable Black American Women,* Smith, Jessie, 1991; *Profiles in Black and White Women,* Chittenden, Elizabeth, 1973; *Running a Thousand Miles to Freedom,* 1850, first edition, Craft, William, second edition, Blackett, R.J.M. 1986; *Underground Rail Road,* Still, William, 1970, Newspapers: *Federal Union,* November 5, 1850; *IBID* November 23, 1856; *IBID* November 26, 1885; *Georgia Journal and Messenger,* June 25, 1885; *Georgia Telegraph,* February 13, 1849.

Chapter 5. Nellie Tayloe Ross: "The First Lady of Wyoming"
Books: *Nellie Tayloe Ross: First Woman Governor,* A Thesis, by Barbara Jean Alaskson, University of Wyoming, Laramie, Wyoming, 1960. Papers: Notes from the Hebbard Collection, University of Wyoming. State Documents: *Address of Nellie Tayloe Ross, Nellie Tayloe Ross: A Biography; Wyoming Labor Journal,* Cheyenne. *The First Woman Gover-*

nor in the First Suffrage State. Department of the Treasury: *Nellie Tayloe Ross Diector of the Mint,* 1972. Magazines: *Good Housekeeping,* Three issues: *The Governor Lady,* 1927; *Family Circle, Nellie Tayloe Ross,* July, 1952; *Westways, The Honorable Nellie,* November, 1976. Newspapers: *Christian Science Monitor,* December 15, 1932, December 20, 1932, August 25, 1935; *Coin World,* November 24, 1976; *Collier's Weekly,* September 25, 1926; *Denver Times,* May 2, 1955, July 27, 1926; *Laramie Republic & Boomerang,* June 19, 1929, November 28, 1997; *Minneapolis Morning Tribune,* May 27, 1929; *Omaha Bee,* July 26, 1925; *Portland, The Maine,* 1925; *Riverton Chronicle,* November, 1976; *Savannah Reporter & Andrew County Democrat,* February 16, 1978; *Wyoming Eagle,* July 5, 1925, August 8, 1926, September 24, 1926, November 17, 1978; *Wyoming State Tribune,* June 16, 1926, November 3, 1926, April 23, 1952.

Chapter 6. May Arkwright Hutton: "An Unconventional Woman"

Books: Fahey, John, *The Days of the Hercules,* 1978; Fargo, Lucile F., *Spokane Story,* 1950; Greenough, Earl S., *The First 100 Years in the Coeur d'Alene Mining District,* 1947; Magnuson, Richard G., *Coeur d'Alene Diaries,* 1968; Montgomery, James W., *Liberated Woman, A Life of May Arkwright Hutton,* 1974; Stole, William, *Silver Strike: The Story of Silver Mining in the Coeur d'Alenes,* 1932. Newspaper articles: *London Times,* Dec., 11, 1910; *New York Times,* May 11, 1910-May 16, 1910; *Spokesman Review,* 1890-1975, assorted articles; *Victoria Daily Times,* June 2, 1910; *Washington News,* April 11, 1910. Special Articles: The May Arkwright Hutton Scrapbooks: Northwest Museum of Arts and Culture, Washington State Historical Society, Spokane, Washington.

Chapter 7. Nellie MacKnight Doyle: The Beloved Lady Doctor of Owens Valley

Books: Smith, Genny, Dr. Nellie: *The Autobiography of Dr. Helen MacKnight Doyle,* first printing, Gotham House, 1934 — reprinted by Genny Smith Books, 1983. Newspapers: *San Francisco Chronicle,* 1937; various newspapers courtesy of Law's Railroad Museum, Bishop, CA; Document: *Dr. Helen MacKnight Doyle,* an autobriography, courtesy of Law's Railroad Museum, Bishop, CA. The story of Dr. Nellie has been made possible through the courtesy of Genny Smith, of Genny Smith Books.

Chapter 8. Klondike Kate: A Legendary Lady

Books: Dickey, R. M., *Gold Fever: A Narrative of the Great Klondike Gold Rush,* 1897-1899, 1997; Hill, Geoff, *Little Known Tales from Oregon History,* 1988; Gilbert, Douglas, *American Vaudeville its Life and Times,* 1940; Lucia, Ellis, *Klondike Kate: The Life and Legend of Kitty Rockwell,* 1972; Morgan, Lael, *Good Time Girls of the Alaskan-Yukon Gold Rush.* 1999; Morgan, Murray, *Skid Row: An Informal Portrait of Skid Row,* 1960; Morrell, Parks, *Lillian Russell,* 1940. Special Sources: Interview, KBND Bend, Oregon, 1955; Book Talk, no date; Historical Gazette, March 1987. Newspapers: *Alaskan Sportsman, The,* August, 1944, October 27, 1946, April, 1947, December, 22, 1959; *Oregonian,* The, Northwest Magazine Section, January 7, and February 4, 1934. Magazines: *American Weekly,* "Klondike Kate's Strange Love Idyll." April 13, 1947; *Life Story Magazine,* "I was Queen of the Klondike," August, 1944.

Books

Alaskan, Barbara Jean A. Thesis: *Nellie Taylor Ross,* 1960

Blackett, R.J.M., *Running a Thousand Miles to Freedom,* William Craft, first printing, reprint, 1986

Child, Lydia, *Notable Black American Women,* 1991

Chitteden, Elizabeth, *Profiles in Black and White,* 1973

Devere, Dorothy, *The Lady of the Rose,* 1993

Dickey, R.M., *Gold Fever: A narrative of the Great Klondike Gold Rush,* 1947

Fahey, John, *The Days of the Hercules,* 1978

Fargo, Lucile F., *Spokane Story,* 1950

Gilbert, Douglas, *American Vaudeville its Life and Times,* 1940

Greenbough, Earl S., *The First Hundred Years in the Coeur d'Alene Mining District,* 1947

Hill, Geoff, *Little Known Tales from Oregon History,* 1988

Lucia, Ellis, *Klondike Kate: The Life and Legend of Kitty Rockwell,* 1972

Montgomery, James W., *Liberated Woman: A Life of May Arkwright Hutton,* 1974

Morgan, Dale, *Jedediah Smith and the Opening of the West,* 1964

Morgan, Lael, *Good Times Girls of the Alaskan-Yukon Gold Rush,* 1999

Morgan, Murray, *Skid Row: An Informal Portrait of Skid Row,* 1960

Morrill, Parks, *Lillian Russell,* 1940

Smith, Genny, *Dr. Nellie: The Autobiography of Dr. Helen MacKnight Doyle,* 1st printing, Gotham House, 1934: reprinted by Genny Smith Books, 1983

Sterling, Dorothy, *Black Foremothers,* 1971

Still, William, *Underground Rail Road,* 1970

Stole, William, *Silver Strike: The Story of Silver Mines in the Coeur d'Alenes,* 1932

Journals

Address, Nellie Tayloe Ross, Wyoming Library Journal, Cheyenne, WY

Biography of Dr. Helen MacKnight Doyle, Laws Railroad and History Museum, Bishop, CA.

Emma Nevada, "The Comstock Nightingale," California Historical Society, Sacramento, CA.

Hebbard Collection, University of Wyoming State Documents

May Arkwright Hutton Scrapbooks, Northwest Museum of Arts & Culture/Eastern Washington State Historical Society, Spokane, WA.

Montana Queen's Experiences as an Indian Captive, Montana Historical Society, Helena, MT.

Women's File, The, Montana Historical Society, Helena, MT

Order these exciting books, by Western author Anne Seagraves, Today!

HIGH-SPIRITED WOMEN OF THE WEST The West is alive! Filled with all the action normally found only in hard-boiled fiction, these true stories bring to life the women who helped shape history. With courage and determination, they left conventional roles behind, becoming America's early feminists. Demanding acceptance on their own terms, these high-spirited women proudly took their place in history beside men of the untamed West. Includes stories of Jessie Benton Fremont, Sarah Winnemucca, Belle Starr, Abigail Duniway and Helen Wiser, the woman who founded Las Vegas.—Autographed—176 pages, illustrated $11.95

WOMEN WHO CHARMED THE WEST These revealing stories tell of the lives and often shocking love affairs of yesterday's leading ladies. Extolled for their beauty and avoiding disgrace by virtue of their charm, these famous actresses livened up an otherwise drab existence as they entertained the Early West. Lillian Russell and Lillie Langtry were glamorous and indiscreet; Adah Issacs Menken, a Victorian rebel, and the delightful Annie Oakley, won the heart of America. This book contains many portraits from famous collections and articles from Annie Oakley's personal scrapbook.—Autographed—176 pages, illustrated $11.95

WOMEN OF THE SIERRA This book offers a touching account of the lives of women achievers from the mid-1800s through the turn-of-the-century. These courageous ladies fought for independence in the male-dominated West, and opened the doors for others to follow. Each woman left her imprint in the Sierra all were important to the West. Stories include Nevada's first woman doctor, the hanging of Juanita, Charlotte "Charley" Parkhurst, stage-driver and Lotta Crabtree, the child "fairy star" of the Sierra. Many of the histories and photos came from the descendents of the women in this heart-warming book.—Autographed—176 pages, illustrated $11.95

SOILED DOVES: PROSTITUTION IN THE EARLY WEST The book every woman should read!—Autographed—176 pages, illustrated $11.95

DAUGHTERS OF THE WEST ROUGH, TOUGH AND IN SKIRTS! These turn-of-the-century gals entered a man's world with a vengeance, many of them conquering it. This action-packed book tells of the women of the Old Wild West who brought a woman's touch to an otherwise uncivilized land.—Autographed—176 pages, illustrated $11.95

To order your own autographed book(s), send a check for $11.95 for each separate title. Postage will be paid by the publisher. Residents of Idaho, please add 5% sales tax.

Mail to: Wesanne Publications
P.O. Box 428
Hayden, Idaho 83835

Thank you for your order!